DEVIL TALK

STORIES

Bilingual Press/Editorial Bilingüe

General Editor
Gary D. Keller

Managing Editor
Karen S. Van Hooft

Associate Editors
Brian Ellis Cassity
Cristina de Isasi
Linda St. George Thurston

Editorial Board
Juan Goytisolo
Francisco Jiménez
Mario Vargas Llosa

Address:
Bilingual Press
Hispanic Research Center
Arizona State University
PO Box 872702
Tempe, Arizona 85287-2702
(480) 965-3867

DEVIL TALK

STORIES

DANIEL A. OLIVAS

Bilingual Press/Editorial Bilingüe
TEMPE, ARIZONA

ISBN 1-931010-27-7

Library of Congress Cataloging-in-Publication Data

Olivas, Daniel A.
    Devil talk : stories / Daniel A. Olivas.
       p. cm
    ISBN 1-931010-27-7
    1. Hispanic Americans—Fiction. 2. California—Social life and customs—Fiction.
3. Mexico—Social life and customs—Fiction. I. Title.

PS3615.L58D48 2004
813'.6—dc22

                                                          2003063889

PRINTED IN THE UNITED STATES OF AMERICA

Front cover art: Devil at Boystown *(1989) by Philip Sydney Field*
Cover and interior design by John Wincek, Aerocraft Charter Art Service

This publication is supported by the Arizona Commission on the Arts with funding from the State of Arizona and the National Endowment for the Arts.

Arizona
Commission
on the Arts

NATIONAL
ENDOWMENT
FOR THE ARTS

Source acknowledgments appear on p. 159.

ACKNOWLEDGMENTS

I once again thank the wonderful folks at Bilingual Press who worked so hard to publish this book. In particular, I am grateful to Gary D. Keller who, after my query, invited me to submit my manuscript. And once again, I am very lucky to have had Linda Thurston as my editor; Linda, you are a writer's dream. I thank Cristina de Isasi, who is responsible for introducing the Press's books to the world; you hit the ground running the moment you started with Bilingual Press and you've been doing a fantastic job ever since.

I thank my parents for their unconditional support of my writing; a son, no matter how old, appreciates having his parents in his corner. So many thanks to my wife, Sue, who, despite her own busy schedule, has made certain that I have time to write my little stories; I love you so much. And of course thanks to our son, Benjamin; you fill our lives with laughter and craziness and we wouldn't think of changing one hair on your head.

*For my wife, Sue,
and our diablito, Benjamin*

Contents

MONK

He liked to do little illegal things. Nothing that hurt anyone, really. But these small acts of defiance, these trifles, made him feel strong, in control, a man to be reckoned with. Or, like Shadrach, Meshach, and Abednego, each time Antonio Reyes did not get caught, he felt that he'd escaped the wrath of the fiery furnace, as if a higher power approved of his defiance and, in turn, protected him. But for Antonio, the golden idol he refused to honor was that web of minor laws and rules that, in his analysis, simply begged to be disobeyed.

Each morning during the work week, for example, after having breakfast with Ruby, his girlfriend of three years, Antonio leaves the massive but beautifully landscaped Summit apartment complex in Woodland Hills, drops by the Starbucks at Victory Boulevard on his way to the Ventura Freeway, orders a cup of coffee (grande drip, half-caf, a little room for cream, please), hops back in his white Camry, eases onto the freeway while drinking his steaming coffee carefully so as to spare his necktie, pulls into the downtown parking garage after an hour's commute (on a good day), grabs his briefcase from the trunk, and starts his day at the Caltrans planning department where he analyzes traffic flows in the southeast grid and writes little reports (that he never sees again) concerning which of Los Angeles's freeways within his grid needs tweaking to improve the average commuter's life. At the end of the day, Antonio snaps his empty briefcase shut, ambles to his car, and, after settling into the driver's seat but before shutting the door, he gently grabs the empty Starbucks cup with his long, elegantly tapered fingertips, furtively looks around the garage, and, seeing that all is clear, places the cup on the oil-stained gray-black asphalt, shuts his door, and starts the car. As he backs out, the tire pops the plastic top off the cup and crushes it along with the cup and the little corrugated insulation sleeve, leaving behind inanimate road kill flattened in a puddle of brown blood. And, as his Camry slides past, Antonio smiles when he sees the results of his little misdemeanor. THOU SHALT NOT LITTER. In third grade, he'd made a poster of the Give-a-Hoot-Don't-Pollute owl shaking his wing at a bad, bad littering boy. Sister Elizabeth gave him an A+ on it. Very nice job, she'd said. Very nice, indeed.

Antonio once made a list of his transgressions. One night, while Ruby slept, he popped a Thelonius Monk CD into his computer and, to the boppy strains of "Well You Needn't," he created a document that delineated, in no particular order, each of his more recent sins (his demarcation line was January 6 two years ago, the day he turned thirty-eight). Before making his list, Antonio experimented with introductory symbols that he wanted to put before each item. He remembered how, on his first day at Caltrans, his new supervisor, Roland, told him his memos could be really "perked up" with such simple markings—"bullets," Roland called them. *Bullets.* Ever since then, Antonio used bullets in his memos. In fact, he became addicted to bullets particularly because the more he used, the more compliments he received from Roland. This private memo needed bullets, too. So Antonio first tried a squiggly line: ~. He didn't care for the look. Too informal. Then he tried a • which is what he used at work, but here it didn't sit right with him. Too dark, too serious, too Catholic. Antonio finally settled on a simple ° because it possessed the elegance of a ~ but with the determination of a •. In any event, after deciding upon the correct bullet, he completed his list, which read as follows:

- Left empty Starbucks cup in parking structure (each evening during work week).
- Ate chocolate-covered almonds (or double-dipped chocolate peanuts) while grocery shopping w/o paying for them (most trips to market).
- Took two *Los Angeles Times* from dispenser while paying for only one (three times, so far); dumped extra copies in apartment recycling bin.
- Took two dollars from Ruby's purse (once).
- From office, took four packs of Post-its (2 in. x 3 in.), one Stanley-Bostitch stapler (black, standard staple), two reams copy paper (generic brand), IBM 3.5-in. diskettes (10 pack), Sanford Major Accent highlighters (2 green, 2 orange, 6 yellow).

Antonio sat back and squinted at his screen. He smiled. "Misterioso" started up. He scratched his small paunch and then rubbed his large biceps to remind himself that he was in pretty good shape for a middle-aged man. When Antonio was satisfied with his list, he deleted it and went to bed.

That night, Antonio dreamt that he was peacefully snoring next to Ruby. He lay on his stomach and enjoyed a delicious deep sleep. Then he felt Ruby's hand just above his tailbone. He grew hard as she rubbed his lower back. Oh, boy! He hadn't had a sex dream in years. He was more than due. But as Ruby rubbed, she began to hurt him. She was digging her thumb in between his vertebrae. Eventually, Ruby punctured Antonio's flesh as she would a succulent orange. *Ouch!* This hurt but he couldn't move. He attempted to wake up by trying to move the index finger of his left hand, which was hanging over the side of the bed, but to no avail. Ruby now had her whole arm in his back and was reaching around inside him! *Ack! Stop, Ruby!* But she didn't because she couldn't hear him. Ah! she finally murmured as she rested her hand on something. What did she have? A Stanley-Bostitch stapler (black, standard staple). Ruby slowly pulled it from Antonio's back with a sickening slurp of torn flesh and blood. What next? Dozens and dozens of smashed, empty Starbucks cups! The plastic tops scraped his wound as she slid them out. And then mounds of chocolate-covered almonds (or double-dipped chocolate peanuts). Several dog-eared copies of the *Los Angeles Times*. Everything! She pulled out each and every one of his little transgressions. When she finished (four packs of Post-its were the last to be salvaged), Antonio came with a heave of his groin as Ruby's hand slipped out of the now-closing hole in his back.

The next morning, before Ruby awoke, Antonio threw his crusty pajama bottoms into the hamper and quickly showered. At breakfast, he watched Ruby eat her granola and read the paper. She was so beautiful! How did he land her? Not only was she fifteen years his junior, but Ruby also raked in 100k as an energetic new attorney with a successful Woodland Hills law firm. Insurance defense. She looked up and smiled.

"What you staring at?"

"You, mi amor. You."

She laughed. "That's what I thought." Ruby leaned forward. "Take a picture, it'll last longer." She took a sip of coffee. "You're dressed pretty casually today."

Antonio looked down at his waffles. "Taking a personal day."

Ruby smiled. "You state employees. Personal holidays. Telecommuting. Fat pensions. And we taxpayers are getting hit in the wallet for it all."

He looked up and returned her smile. "Yes, mi amor, but I make half of what you do. You could always become a state attorney, if you wanted. Fewer hours. Great benefits. The Ronald Reagan Building is only a few blocks away from my office. We could have lunch together every day."

Ruby inhaled her coffee's aroma. "By the way, you have to drop by your parents' house today. I've finished reviewing their will. I've made some markings on it. They should raise these issues with their lawyer."

Antonio rubbed his chin. "Where is it?"

"By your keys."

"Does it have to be today?"

"They're your parents. You're a big boy. Do what you want. I've done my duty."

"Yes, you have."

"They love me, you know."

"Yes, they do."

"More than they love you, no doubt."

Antonio snorted. "I'm sure they love you more. You're perfect. Me, I'm an ingrate."

"No, Tony. You just don't know how good they are. What they gave you and all."

"That's what I mean. Nothing but an ingrate."

"Anyway, there are some pretty big holes in the will that should be plugged. I would have written the whole thing for them but they refused. Had to spend their limited money on some solo practitioner who goes to their church."

"Yes, my parents are stupid people."

"Shut up. I'm not criticizing them, really. It's actually very sweet."

"They're sweet, stupid people, then. And I'm an ingrate."

"Yes, you are. But you're my ingrate."

Antonio stood up, walked over to Ruby, and leaned his chin on the top of her head. He could smell her strawberry shampoo.

"Why do I love you, Tony?"

"Because I'm a certified genius."

"No, that's not it. Besides, I haven't seen the certificate yet."

"It's in the mail."

"Why do I love you?"

"It's because of the massive slabs of muscle I've developed at the gym. That, and my huge schlong."

"Ah," Ruby sighed as Antonio moved his hands to her breasts. "That's the reason. Your huge schlong. I forgot about that."

"How could you?" he said softly. Ruby closed her eyes as Antonio rubbed her nipples through her silk blouse. His dream popped back into his head and he grew harder. "Can you stay a little longer?"

Ruby pulled forward so that Antonio's hands had to slide off her. "I wish, Tony. I wish. But I've got this appellate argument in two days and I'm doing a little moot court today with the partners."

Antonio sighed. "Are you sure?" He sounded pitiful to himself.

She stood up and snuggled up to him. "Sorry, mi amor. Sorry."

"Me too."

*   *   *

After Ruby had left, Antonio called his parents. They weren't home, thank God. He left a short message. Now, what to do with his personal day? Work out. Yes. First, a good workout. Antonio quickly changed into a ragged Loyola High School T-shirt and baggy shorts. After jumping into the car and buckling up, he went through his cassette case and chose Bebel Gilberto's new CD. Ruby had given it to him for Valentine's Day to, as she put it, freshen up his music collection. She was getting a bit tired of Antonio's Monk as well as Stan Getz, Tito Puente, and Miles Davis. Ruby didn't see the irony in her present, however: Bebel is João Gilberto's daughter, and João, of course, sang with Astrud Gilberto on Stan Getz's bossa nova hit "The Girl from Ipanema." *Ah! It all connects. Like the L.A. freeway system.* He enjoyed the haunting voice of Bebel as he took Van Owen to Platt, which became Sherman Way. The parking lot at the Spectrum Club was unusually busy.

Damn! Hopefully there would be a recumbent bike for him. He grabbed his weather-beaten copy of *Crime and Punishment* (he's going to finish it, this time, dammit!), and trotted into the gym. As one of the young men behind the desk scanned his membership card, Antonio heard one of the female trainers chatting with the manager. The trainer, whose blond pony tail bounced happily at the top of her head, was pretty only because she was young, or so Antonio surmised. He figured that in about ten or fifteen years, her plain, broad face and little body would disintegrate into those of another chubby housewife living in the Valley with an SUV and too much time on her hands.

"Today *I'm* going to be the sunshine that isn't out *there*," she said in a too-loud chirp. She was right, thought Antonio. Not that she's going to be a little ray of sunshine for the sweaty patrons at the Spectrum Club, but that it was rather cloudy outside, which he hadn't really noticed. As Antonio headed toward the weight room, Little Miss Sunshine kept chirping about how everyone needed to smile to chase those clouds away. Antonio moved into a jog just to escape her voice.

Once safely in the weight room, he scanned the area where the stationary bicycles stood like squat metallic soldiers in front of several enormous overhead TVs. Too damn crowded today. Was there a bike for him? He squinted a bit because he hated to work out wearing his glasses. Ah! A free one, at the end by the StairMasters. Antonio almost skipped to it and settled into a cushioned seat with a sigh. He programmed the bicycle for thirty minutes at a level grade, level five resistance. He cracked his book and started to read Raskolnikov's rant about his sister's suitor. But Ruby's question from this morning ran through his mind. *Why does she love me? Why would she ask? Am I lovable?* Antonio looked around. He saw a few young, handsome guys who could easily steal Ruby away if they had a steady job and some kind of college degree. Those were important to Ruby. And why shouldn't they be? But the question of his age arose in his mind: *When she's thirty-five, I'll be fifty. When she's forty-five, I'll be sixty! Yikes!* As he became mired in this math, he inadvertently kept his gaze on one particular young man doing a military press. The guy suddenly noticed Antonio, and smiled very, very broadly. *Oops! Have to read this book.* Antonio quickly buried his nose in Raskolnikov's troubles.

Antonio went home and showered. He usually felt refreshed after a good workout, but right now he only felt drained. Indeed, Antonio noticed that he looked pale. After drying and dressing, he saw that the answering machine was flashing at him, so he played the new message.

"Mijo," the thin, old voice said. "We're home now. Come on by anytime. Your father and I would love to see you. And thank Ruby for all her hard work."

Antonio sighed. He grabbed his wallet, the marked-up will, and the car keys and drove in a sulk to his parents' house. On the way there, he felt as if a chunk of the freeway were sitting on his chest. He tried to calm himself by breathing deeply the way Ruby had taught him. *Imagine a peaceful scene whenever you feel stressed out,* she had told him. *Like what?* he had asked. *Imagine you're lying on a blanket on a deserted beach, the wonderful warm sun is relaxing every muscle, and the waves are hitting the sand in a perfect rhythm.* And her simple little idea had worked! So as he got on the freeway and headed to his parents', Antonio thought about this peaceful scene and breathed deeply. He imagined, as best he could while driving, a deserted Venice Beach, the one he always went to when he was young. With each deep breath, the image of the stretch of perfect, peaceful beach became clearer and clearer until it was fixed in his mind in sharp focus. He saw himself lying on his belly soaking up the warm, nurturing sun. The waves licked the sand in a teasing, almost erotic way. Ah! The weight on Antonio's chest began to lift, ever so slowly, and easy breathing became his friend, his confidant, his lover. But something was wrong. The waves came closer with each crash on the shore. The warm foam touched his hand. The water now tickled his ear. Yikes! In no time, Antonio's head was submerged! Stop! Despite vicious honks from a black SUV, he pulled over to the freeway's shoulder. *Screw the beach*, he thought. *Screw it.*

Antonio finally made it to his parents' house. He pulled into their driveway, got out, and peered about the old neighborhood. There had not been many changes since he was a kid except that it felt crowded and somewhat dingier. He worked his way over the unevenly laid brick walkway that his parents had put down with their own hands when he was no more than ten. Antonio had not even rested his foot on the cement porch's first step before his mother opened the heavy 1920s-style oak door.

"¡Mi cielo!" she cried in what sounded to Antonio like a dog's yelp.

"Hi, Mom."

"Come, come. I have some nice albóndigas for you." She gave him a tight hug and kissed his chin, which required her to stand on her toes.

I hate albóndigas, thought Antonio. "Thank you, Mom. No one can make albóndigas like you do. Not even Abuelita could."

They entered the kitchen and the soup's heavy aroma overtook Antonio's senses. He felt dizzy. "Please sit," his mother said. "Your father will be down in a second. He was napping."

Antonio sat at the round table and immediately grabbed a paper napkin to fiddle with. "He's napping a lot these days, isn't he?"

"Mijo," laughed his mother, "he's almost eighty. What do you expect?" She walked over to a large, steaming pot and ladled out a generous serving of albóndigas into a cracked brown bowl. With great care, she brought it to Antonio. "Eat up!"

"Mom, he's only seventy-four. He's not almost eighty."

"He'll be eighty before you know it," she answered as she poured three cups of coffee in such rapid succession that Antonio was taken aback for a moment. She stirred in a large helping of cream and handed him a mug that had a picture of a happy Santa Claus on one side and a smiling reindeer on the other. "Before you know it!" As these last words fell from her mouth, Antonio's father appeared as if by magic.

"Before I know what?" said his father.

"Pop!" Antonio stood up and hugged his father. He felt bony and small to Antonio and smelled slightly sour, unwashed. He didn't hug Antonio back.

"Sit, Tony. Sit." Antonio released his father and sat with a snort.

After some silence while his father settled into a chair, Antonio pulled out a wad of paper from his shirt pocket. "I brought the will," he tried to declare triumphantly, but instead sounded apologetic. "Ruby made some comments in the margins."

"Ah! Ruby!" exclaimed his father. "How is that pretty lady?"

Antonio looked down at his cup of coffee. The cream still swirled about. "Fine. Making big bucks."

"The money's not important," said his mother as she sat down. "You make plenty."

Antonio didn't like the direction of the conversation. His hands grew moist and he could feel the perspiration beading up on his scalp. "So, Pops," he said, "the car running okay?"

"You certainly do make plenty enough money," said his father. "Enough to buy a nice casa, enough to start a familia."

"Your Papá did it on a lot less," offered his mother. "He drove a bus his whole life and we never wanted, did we?"

"I *want* a family," Antonio almost whispered.

"El que mucho habla, poco logra," snorted his father. "You have to act if you want something."

Antonio took a great gulp of coffee and burned his mouth in the process. Ever since his divorce from Leticia six years ago, which had required the selling of his small but beautiful North Hollywood home, his parents never lost a chance to push for another stab at marriage because, after all, what is old age without the joy of grandchildren? The responsibility had weighed heavily on Antonio's shoulders since his baby sister, Ana, had died as a sophomore at Brown. They called it an accident but Antonio couldn't figure out how someone could accidentally wash down a whole bottle of sleeping pills with a tumbler of Jack Daniel's.

"Look," Antonio began, "she's not ready."

"She?" said his father. "You're the one who is supposed to ask. You should be ready to do that. You're the hombre."

"If you asked, she'd say yes," smiled his mother. "How could she not?"

Antonio looked around the kitchen helplessly. The back of his shirt was drenched. He noticed Diablo, the old Siamese cat, dozing on the TV while Oprah mutely discussed a novel with its author, a white, bald, bearded man who smiled and nodded just a bit too much. *If only I could be Diablo and sleep the day away,* he thought. *Now, that would be a wonderful existence.*

"Leticia was a mistake," continued his mother. "We told you that from the beginning but we stayed out of it after you made up your mind. Ruby, on the other hand. ¡Ay! We couldn't ask for a sweeter girl!"

Antonio wanted to tell his mother that Ruby was indeed a sweet girl. So sweet that she let him have anal sex with her every so often.

"Yes, she's sweet," sighed Antonio, keeping his eyes on Oprah. His mother tapped his arm and he turned to her.

"We only want the best for you," she said. His father nodded.

How can they know what's best for me if I don't know what's best for me? He let his eyes wander first over his mother's face, and then his father's. *Who are these old people?* He didn't recognize them as they sat around the trusty round mahogany table that Antonio and his sister used to play under even though he was several years older than she. His father was never very imposing, physically, that is: he was always small-boned and waiflike, and age only exaggerated this trait. His mother was built similarly, though she had large hands and feet, too large for her little frame. From the beginning (and other than his mother's hands and feet), they looked like fraternal twins, with large brown eyes and perpetual half-smiles that looked as if they had just been crying but were trying to be good troopers. Standing together, they reminded Antonio of novelty ceramic salt-and-pepper shakers, the kind you'd find at any of the dozen or so antique shops that ran along Sherman Way between Shoup Avenue and Topanga Canyon Boulevard. They weren't really idiots, of course; Antonio just liked to say that to push Ruby's buttons. They read more than most and were up on the new movies. And his parents always voted, which was something Antonio had given up long ago. The most embarrassing thing about his parents was that, in the end, they were remarkably ordinary when compared to the characters who inhabited the old neighborhood. Antonio simply didn't know how he came from them, out of their lovemaking. They had tried to raise Antonio to be a good man, a man who would do what they did: marry and raise a family. But they seemed to have failed in this one true mission of their simple lives.

"Leticia was not right for you," his mother repeated.

Antonio almost jumped. "What?" he asked.

"Your mother said that Leticia was never right for you."

They spoke the truth. Where Leticia was small-minded, voluptuous, and content to work at the Ralph's checkout stand, Ruby was well-traveled, petite, and on the fast track to partnership. Leticia's clever and energetic ways in bed had made Antonio stupid so that when the marriage finally fell apart under its own weight, all he could think about was not being able to sleep with her again.

"How you married her we'll never know," said his father.

She screwed my brains out, that's how, Pops. But he couldn't say such a thing. "Nobody's perfect, Pops," Antonio offered instead. "Especially me."

After a silence, his mother said, "Please eat your albóndigas. They're getting cold."

"Yes, Mom," Antonio said. He took a spoonful. "Delicious."

"Anything for mijo," she said. "Anything."

⋆   ⋆   ⋆

That night, after cooking a wonderful dinner for Ruby and then making love, Antonio fell into a deep sleep. At first, he floated through a nondescript, peaceful dream in which he watched the clouds sway to Monk's amiable "Ruby, My Dear" as the mid-afternoon sun warmed his skin with gentle kisses. He then realized that he was walking down a deserted Western Avenue toward Pico Boulevard not far from his parents' home. The warm sun grew warmer as his walk soon became a trudge, with each step becoming more difficult, as if his shoes were slowly filling with lead. Monk's tune changed suddenly to "Straight, No Chaser," and Antonio felt wooden handles aching in his sweaty hands. And then, without warning, a *crack!* of a whip came down hard on his back. He winced and fell to one knee.

"Get up, you bastard!" cried a hard, somewhat familiar male voice from behind.

Antonio realized that the handles were those of some kind of wagon. He tried to turn but couldn't move his neck. Another crack of the whip made Antonio stand and start pulling the wagon again.

"You lazy bastard!" yelled the unseen man.

Antonio lifted his head toward the now-hot asphalt and saw his parents, Ruby, and his late sister standing in a huddle.

"Don't hurt my boy!" yelled his mother through tears.

"Antonio, my love! Don't lose your spirit!" Ruby cried.

"Listen to Ruby!" offered his father.

Antonio's sister was the only one who didn't say a word. She simply stood there, looking radiant and with a faint smile.

Crack! And this time Antonio fell to both knees.

"Get up!" yelled the man. "Get up or I'll kill you!"

"You can't!" cried his mother. "It's illegal to kill a man!"

Antonio could hear the man jump from the wagon and land on the asphalt with a loud thud of work boots. "He's bought and paid for!" answered the man. "He's goddamned mine and I can kill him if I want!"

The man let Antonio feel his fury with a rhythmic whipping that, with each contact, made Antonio shrink into himself in unyielding pain. Though near death, he wanted to see the face of his torturer. With great effort, Antonio turned his head and, after a moment or two and through blood that ran down his forehead, he saw the man.

"You!" yelled Antonio. "It's you!"

The man who stood over Antonio was Antonio himself. A younger version, yes, but clearly it was his own face that he looked into. And with a last crack of the whip, Antonio woke with a jump. Ruby stirred. The blue light of the clock showed that he had been asleep no more that an hour. Antonio strained his eyes and could see the soft outline of Ruby's peaceful, beautiful face. He touched it gently before getting out of bed and heading to the bathroom. He shut the door before turning on the light so as not to disturb Ruby. He closed the toilet seat, sat, and rubbed his face with both hands.

It was an unusually warm night, so they kept the small, high bathroom window open. Antonio looked up and, even without his glasses, he could see a bright moon hidden by a bit of cloud. He stood and walked to the window. The crickets were so loud that he thought they could be in the room with him. A faraway ambulance rushed to an unknown destination. Antonio reached to scratch his chin but stopped short with a sharp pain that ran from the middle of his back to the top of his shoulder. He slowly continued the movement of his arm and his hand eventually reached his chin. Antonio scratched hard.

"Tony?"

Antonio turned. Ruby stood in the doorway wearing only a very short T-shirt. He had been so lost in the moon and the crickets that he hadn't heard the door open. "Yes?" he said.

"You okay?" she said without moving into the bathroom.

Antonio closed the window and walked to her. "I'm fine, mi amor. Perfectly fine."

He slid his hands around Ruby's tiny waist and rested his open palms on the small of her back. He smelled her tousled hair before kissing her head.

"Are you sure?" she said as she rested her head on his chest.

"I couldn't be better," he answered. "Couldn't be better."

"Thank you," she said.

"For what?"

"For seeing your parents. Your mother called after you left their place."

"You didn't tell me. We had all dinner to talk."

Ruby pulled back and sat on the closed toilet. "I forgot."

"So?"

"So what?"

Antonio opened the window and searched for the moon but the cloud had completely devoured it. "What did Mom say?"

Ruby rubbed her red eyes. "Oh, that you're a wonderful boy and when are we going to get married and give them grandchildren."

Antonio jumped and turned to her. "What? She said what?"

She laughed. "Well, she didn't say all that exactly. But I could read between the lines. I'm a brilliant lawyer, remember?"

Antonio let out a little laugh. "What did you say?"

"I told her that you were wonderful and that I loved you."

"And?"

"There should be more?" Ruby laughed.

Antonio returned the laugh. "Let's go to bed."

"About time you asked," Ruby said as she slowly stood. She put her arm around Antonio's waist and guided him toward the bedroom as if he were a child. "Bedtime for Bonzo."

"Bedtime for Bonzo," Antonio said. "Bedtime for Bonzo."

*   *   *

Later that night, Antonio dreamt that Ruby was trying to put her thumb into his back again. But this time, there was no music. And it felt different. Sharp. Like she was pushing a bit of plastic in between his vertebrae. He realized that she was, indeed, pushing a cracked plastic coffee lid into what started as a little hole in his back but which eventually opened wide like a baby's mouth ready for a spoonful of Gerber's applesauce. The lid finally slid in with an aching little slurp. Next she pushed in dozens of smashed empty Starbucks cups, and then the Stanley-Bostitch stapler. Each intrusion hurt more than the last. The copies of the *Los Angeles Times* were a mess to insert but she did. The easiest were the chocolate-covered almonds and double-dipped chocolate peanuts because they simply slipped in without catching on skin.

When Ruby had finished filling Antonio with his little transgressions, the hole slowly closed until he felt nothing but a little burning sensation. In his dream, Ruby kissed the small of his back and then rolled over to sleep. Antonio awoke. Ruby lay beside him in precisely the way she appeared to sleep in his dream. He touched her hair; it tickled his fingertips. Antonio smiled and nestled his head deeply into the pillow but kept his eyes on Ruby. He murmured, "Ruby, Ruby," like a mantra. Within a few minutes, he fell into a deep, dreamless sleep.

WILLIE

ilfredo likes to dress to get Papá all riled up. You know, Willie wears those short-shorts that you see on the ladies who walk up and down that bad street near the Shell Station that Mamá says no self-respecting good Catholic would wander by unless your car died and you needed to get some help from Manny who works there. Mamá says those putas have no right to mess up our nice neighborhood. But the neighborhood don't look so nice and I figure some pretty ladies walking up and down a street can only make things look nice, right?

So Willie likes to put on these short-shorts that are so tiny that his nalgas are hanging out and then he pops in these blue contacts so that his eyes look like he's out of some scary space movie where only one person knows that the aliens are taking over people's bodies and no one, not even your father, believes you when you say they're going to take us over, too. I hate those movies. They make my stomach hurt.

Anyway, today Willie comes down the stairs looking so pretty with his long legs showing and his eyes not looking scary this time for some reason but shining a blue that looks like Uncle Kiko's restored Mustang instead of a space alien's eyes. And I think to myself that Willie's cheeks even look special, kind of red like a flower, like the blush Mamá finally let me buy from Sav-On even though I'm only twelve but she says, mija, you're a good girl so it's okay. I think Willie likes to take a little of my blush every so often because I see big fingerprints in it that are bigger than mine but that's okay because I think he looks prettier than me anyway so he should

17

use it. So this morning here comes Willie looking really extra pretty and Papá is reading *La Opinión* at the breakfast table, drinking his hot black coffee after finishing a nice big bowl of menudo, which is his special treat on Sunday mornings.

Willie sits down at the table without saying nothing. Mamá is busy at the stove, cleaning something up, I don't know what. I'm on the floor watching the *Powerpuff Girls* video on the small TV that sits on the kitchen counter near all the Coke cans for recycling. I look up and smile at Willie. Willie reaches across the table and grabs a piece of pan dulce and these little gold chains that hang from his wrist just jingle-jangle and they remind me of Christmas which is a mile away. Willie gives me a wink and I smile and look at Papá who is now looking up at Willie but Papá isn't smiling and so my smile falls from my face like a dirty sock. I don't like Papá's eyes right now. They're all squinted-up and his big black eyebrows come down in a mean "V" and he puts his coffee cup down on the green place mat and some of it spills over the sides of the cup but Papá doesn't seem to care.

Finally, Papá says, ¿Qué es esto?

What's what? Willie says through a mouthful of pan dulce.

I turn to look at my video again but not for long. Mamá screams and my head swivels like a chair and I see Papá holding Willie against the wall and something doesn't look right because Willie is looking down at Papá even though Willie is shorter by about six inches and then I see that Willie's feet aren't touching the floor no more, they're just dangling there like a doll's feet and I notice for the first time that he's wearing these pretty clear-plastic sandals. And I don't know what to do so I just sit there with tears coming down my face like someone just turned on the backyard hose and Mamá isn't moving, too, but now she isn't screaming, just standing in the kitchen, hands pulling at the dishrag, mouth open like an empty can of tuna and eyes owl-wide.

And Papá starts to yell something in Spanish so fast I don't know what he's saying. And then I see Willie's pretty, fake blue eyes flicker toward me. And he smiles. Not a big smile. Just enough so that I know he's smiling at me. And suddenly my tears turn off. Just like that. And the house seems so quiet now, like we're suddenly under water, but I see Papá's lips moving fast like a cat. And Willie just hangs there against the wall, smiling at me. Looking pretty.

BENDER

his will not do, says Raúl. No, this will not do at all.
Raúl stands up, pushing back his chair with the insides of his knees. He stands before the table for a moment with his hands on his hips.

No, this cannot be left as it is, Raúl says.

He turns on his heel and marches barefoot toward the bedroom. Raúl shakes his head from side to side. This will not do at all.

He finds María sitting on their bed cutting her toenails with a large pair of clippers that she purchased last year at the Santa Monica Pier. On one side of the clippers, the part you put your thumb on, is an elongated version of the Mexican flag with the eagle looking as though it has been stretched out like Silly Putty. A flailing serpent hangs from the eagle's beak and looks like an evil penis or a goose's neck. María lets her nail clippings fly up and land throughout the rumpled sheets of the unmade bed. She wears no clothes and sits with her left leg out, her right leg bent, and her foot pulled up close to her face. Perspiration drips from her face and rains on her round, firm toes. The Los Angeles summer sun shines hard and heartlessly through the large window and lights up the bed like a Broadway stage. María smells ripe and delicious to Raúl, but he has some other business to take care of right then. Otherwise, he would pull off his boxers and slide across the sheets and put himself into María.

Have you seen it? Raúl asks María.

Yes.

Well?

Well what, mi cielo?

She clips the nail on her big toe and a hard crescent moon flies up and almost hits Raúl on his knitted brow.

Raúl scratches his small, hairy belly and then his head and then his belly again because scratching his belly feels more appropriate at that moment.

What should we do about it? he continues. It presents a problem, doesn't it?

Donde una puerta se cierra, otra se abre, says María without looking up.

How does this present an opportunity? asks Raúl in all sincerity but getting a little irritated.

El que mucho habla, poco logra, she answers, spreading out her right leg and pulling her left foot up toward her face. Her wavy black hair tickles the tips of her toes and she laughs a little before starting to clip the next set of toenails.

You're right, says Raúl. Enough talk. Time to act. He turns and walks back to the kitchen table.

By the time he gets there, it has moved from one corner of the table to the other. Raúl pulls his chair under him and sits down with a little grunt. Perspiration drips from both armpits and down his sides.

Okay, says Raúl. Look at me.

It turns and looks at Raúl.

Okay, begins Raúl. Let's deal with this now or else I can't get on with my day and I have a lot of plans, you know.

It looks at Raúl with large sorrowful eyes and Raúl fears that it will start crying at any moment if he doesn't watch his tone.

Do you understand me? asks Raúl in a softer voice.

It nods slowly.

María yells from the bedroom, Ask it if it's hungry, mi cielo.

No! yells Raúl without moving his eyes from it. That will defeat the purpose. But as Raúl says this, it lets a tear drop slowly first from one eye and then the other.

Okay, okay, says Raúl. Are you hungry?

It nods and smiles displaying many sharp little teeth.

Okay. Raúl stands up and walks over to the refrigerator and opens it. This is what we have, says Raúl. We have apple-sauce, bread, flour tortillas, grape jam (not jelly), fat-free half & half (how is that possible?), Egg Beaters, and Diet Coke.

It makes a snide comment.

I know, I know, answers Raúl. I have a cholesterol problem.

It asks a question.

My LDL is way too high and HDL too low, says Raúl.

It asks another question.

Of course I work out, answers Raúl.

It says something.

Well, I'm glad your numbers are good. Okay, says Raúl in exasperation. If you don't make a choice, I'll choose for you.

It makes a choice.

Good, says Raúl and he grabs the applesauce, shuts the refrigerator door with a flick of his wrist, and grabs a spoon and bowl from the cupboard. He sets it all on the table, scoops a large spoonful of the applesauce, and plops it into the bowl. There, he says. Eat up.

It lets out a little laugh before sticking its tongue into the applesauce.

María walks into the room still naked, but her toenails are nicely clipped. Her chocolate skin shines with perspiration.

Well, she says. What's up?

Raúl looks at María. Her wide brown hips and the large inverted triangle of black hair between her muscular thighs make Raúl hard and he quickly sits down before María and it are able to notice.

María, Raúl says. Get a robe on or something. The windows are open.

María yawns and stretches her arms up over her head. This makes her breasts bounce just a little. Raúl grows harder.

María, please, says Raúl. For me.

El tiempo perdido no se recupera jamás, she says with a lascivious smile and walks slowly to the bedroom.

I know, says Raúl. But this is not the time. I need to deal with it.

It is still lapping up the applesauce while making a sound that is a cross between a purr and a dentist's drill.

María comes back into the kitchen wearing a tiny Mel Tormé T-shirt but her bottom is still naked. She plops down on one of the chairs and leans close to it while it slurps the applesauce. The perspiration on her buttocks makes it difficult to shift on the vinyl seat cushion without her skin sticking and making an unpleasant sound.

It's very nice, María says.

That's not the point, says Raúl. It will grow, like the other one, and then we're going to have trouble. Don't you remember?

El que no arriesga, no pasa el charco, she mumbles, avoiding Raúl's eyes.

You're full of dichos this morning, Raúl says. It's not a matter of taking risks or gaining anything. We already know what's going to happen if we don't deal with it now.

Raúl turns to it. Finished? he asks it.

It nods, wiping applesauce from its large pink lips.

Ask its name, says María.

You're here. You ask it.

What's your name? asks María.

It answers and smiles at María's breasts.

I like that name, says María. Bender. Bender.

It's a stupid name, says Raúl.

It laps up the last of the applesauce, ignoring Raúl's insult.

Oh, look! It finished, says María.

Good, says Raúl. Time to go.

It opens its eyes as wide as it can.

Time to go, repeats Raúl. María feels a pang of sadness.

It looks at Raúl. It looks at María. It lets out a sigh. Slowly and with great effort, it leaps from the table and lands on the hardwood floor with a thump. Raúl and María do not move. It shuffles to the front door and manages to open it. It lurks in the doorway for a moment looking forlorn.

Well? asks Raúl. What are you waiting for?

It sighs before turning and slamming the door behind itself. The sound reverberates throughout the room.

Raúl and María sit silently staring at the closed door.

There, says Raúl. It's done.

Yes, says María. It's done.

María stands up and walks back to the bedroom. The floorboards creak under her bare feet. It's done, she says again.

Raúl sits at the kitchen table with his hands folded as if in prayer. A gardener starts up his leaf blower and the motorized roar invades the apartment through the open windows like a reckless burglar. After a few minutes, Raúl stands and picks up the empty bowl and places it gently into the sink. He then closes the applesauce jar and puts it back into the refrigerator.

It's done, he says again to no one in particular. Raúl turns and walks to the bedroom where María already lies in bed waiting for him. The floorboards creak under his bare feet.

EURT

Patrick, boy, is this thing on? I can't tell. They get smaller all the time. Let me see that. Don't worry, I won't hurt it. Toshiba? Japanese? Used to be that when something didn't work, we'd say it was made in Japan. Not anymore. What? Oh, yeah. Where do you want it? Okay. Should I lean into it when I talk? No? Okay, Patrick. What do you want me to talk about for this, what do you call it? Oral history? You kids sure like those old stories. I know it's for a grade, but admit you like this shit. Oh, sorry. I'll watch it. Okay, which story do you want? No, not that. Too personal. What else? Really? The St. Francis Dam? Sure. Suit yourself. Don't know what kind of grade you'll get, but I'll oblige because you're my favorite grandchild. Don't laugh. It's true.

Okay, here goes. As I've told you before, not many of us know why Eurt's mother named him Eurt. Strange name. Pronounced "yurt" like the word "hurt" but with a "y." Certainly not a name you could find in the Bible, nor is it a name befitting a Mexican child. Well, actually, part Mexican. Because Eurt's mother was not Mexican but some kind of white maybe with a little Pueblo Indian mixed in her, or so some of us figured. The old women who knew Sarah said she came from New Mexico. She had these high cheekbones and Asian eyes and she was topped off with glistening red-blond hair that she kept in two tightly wound braids cascading like

27

a waterfall down her back. So the old women said she must have Pueblo blood mixed in with maybe Irish or English or maybe even Swedish or German. Too beautiful and strange for her own good, the old women clicked through their toothless, puckered gums. And the men. Shit. Oh, sorry. I mean, "shoot." Better?

Anyways, the men couldn't get enough eyefuls of Sarah. All the men. White, Negro, Chinese, Mexican. All the men. But only one man, Alfonso Villa—a distant cousin of the great Pancho Villa—made any kind of impression on Sarah. Which is a shame. Because if Sarah had fallen in love with any other man, even me, she'd probably be alive today. She'd be as old as me. But you know women live longer than men, usually. And that whole horrible incident with Eurt never would've happened. But you can't rewrite history, and you never can figure when one act—one innocent and even good act—might set in motion a series of happenings that end up creating an evil result. Evil. That's the only word for what happened.

It was May 1927 when Alfonso and I first saw Sarah. We were working the farms near the Santa Clara River, around Saugus not too far from the San Francisquito Canyon—Six Flags Magic Mountain is around there now, I think—and we were living in a makeshift camp set up cheap for us workers. Mostly Mexican and some Chinese. Could see the St. Francis Dam from where we slept. Smelly place. And goddamn dusty. Sorry, but there is no other way to say it. Goddamn dusty. You can edit that later, Patrick. Anyways, though I'm white, I lived for almost ten years in Chihuahua when my papa dragged me and my older sister Elsie out of Dallas away from my crazy mother. Papa just wanted to get us the hell out of the state, out of the goddamn country because Mama was dangerous and who knows what she would have done to her two children. See this scar here? Mama put the edge of a hot frying pan there just to teach me not to talk back. Well, that was the last straw. So Papa saw fit to take us away.

The years passed—ten to be exact—and Papa fashioned leather goods for a living. And me and Elsie lived just like the Mexicans. Even went to a school run by priests even though we're Protestant, at least by tradition. After we got word that Mama died sometime in spring of 1924, we came back north because Papa just missed this country. But he wanted something new. So we settled in California by the Santa Clara River. Poor Elsie died a year later of influenza and Papa followed her just a half year after that. There was just me. And I didn't give a good goddamn what I did for a living as long as I made enough to eat, drink, and buy some time with a good whore now and again. Sorry. Edit that if you want.

When Alfonso and I first saw Sarah, I'd been working the Fredrickson farm for almost three years. Seasonal work, you know. But it kept me with the right amount of money for my needs. I was nineteen and he was twenty-one or two. Anyway, Alfonso and I had worked a long day and we were having some good beer at this little bar with this big sign over the front door that said THE TIN ROOF. It mostly catered to us farm workers but a lot of other folks came on in because it had good prices and some decent food, too. Alfonso and I had hit it off pretty good the year before because I'd lived in Chihuahua, like I said, and he had lots of relatives on his mother's side who still lived there. My Spanish was good and his English was even better. So we were as close as we could be not being related or anything. We were drinking to that Lindbergh fellow who landed in Paris two days before. Everyone was so proud even though most of us couldn't figure how what he did could help us in any way. All the Mexicans and Chinese toasted him. So we lifted our glasses and said, "To Lindy," which is what they were calling that young man. The papers said his mother was so proud that she couldn't find words to express her joy. And President Coolidge sent some kind of congratulations through that embassy in Paris saying how the flight crowned the record of American aviation, whatever that means.

The funniest thing though, the part I like because I remember how hot and dirty I used to get back then—even sixty years' distance hasn't made me forget—the newspapers said that Lindy was escorted to the embassy after landing and then fighting the crowds. He was in real need of a bath. So the American Ambassador's son took Lindy to a room at the embassy where a hot bath waited. Before dipping into the tub, Lindy drinks some port and then some milk. Papers said Lindbergh relaxed for a real long time before he got out, combed his hair, put on a pair of flowered silk pajamas, a silk bathrobe and—I like this part—Moroccan leather slippers. All this compliments of the ambassador's son. And he gave a few newspaper interviews dressed just like that. I will never forget that story.

Patrick, need a drink or something? Pepsi, the kind you like? Okay. Just offering.

So, anyways, here it was Tuesday night and we were hot and tired and getting a little drunk and toasting Lindbergh's landing in Paris and in walks this woman through the front doors. Beautiful. Alfonso's head swivels so fast I think it's going to come off. He had a nose, he did. Almost like radar. Beautiful woman within striking distance, Alfonso had his eyes trained on her within two seconds. Goddamn amazing skill, that. We stood at the bar which, if truth be told, was nothing more than a wide board set on bricks on either end with a white tablecloth thrown over it to make it look nicer than it was. She came in and quickly glanced around. Sarah looked in a hurry or something. Nervous. I know why now but then, she looked as though she had lost something and needed to find it *pronto*.

Well, she eventually looks over to the bar and spies me and Alfonso. I kind of push my hair back off my forehead and straighten up some. I was foolish for women back then. Too old now. Alfonso? Well, he was a cool character. He was handsome and he knew it. Looked like his cousin, the great Pancho

Villa, except even more handsome with smooth, brown skin like a baby's butt. Thick head of curly black hair. Neat little mustache. I'm no queer or nothing, but he was the handsomest man I'd ever seen. So Sarah eventually rests her eyes on him and it was over, I tell you. I had no chance in hell. She suddenly looks calmer, like she found what she was looking for even though Alfonso never saw her before in his life and vice-versa. Sarah saunters on over to us, smiling now, and sidles up to Alfonso. She orders a Coca-Cola and then just stands there waiting for the inevitable. Alfonso gives me a little wink and then turns to Sarah.

"How are you?" he asks her in almost perfect English. And she doesn't even turn to him. Can you believe it? She looks the other way at the window or something and doesn't answer. Alfonso gives me a quick glance and smiles this little sly smile. This is going to be fun, he's thinking. I can tell he's going to play the game. Now, Sarah is wearing this very pretty Mexican dress. You know, the long white cotton ones with pretty embroidery. It's a little loose on her but she looks beautiful. Her hair is perfectly braided and it glistens in the lamplight. Other men and even the women start to notice her.

Anyways, Alfonso tries something else. He says, "Señorita, let me introduce myself and my friend. I am Alfonso Villa and this is my very fine friend, James O'Hara."

Alfonso always became real formal when he got nervous. She turns and smiles with these white teeth and I could see Alfonso's knees buckle just a little. Even for him, Sarah's beauty could make him get weak.

She says, "I'm Sarah García. But people call me Tootsie." Funny, isn't it? Tootsie! Like that goddamn movie with that little actor, what's his name? Yeah. Hoffman. But, that's what she said. And we both smiled like idiots. So we kind of . . . what? Oh. Okay. Turn that tape over and I'll go take a pee if that's okay with you, Patrick boy.

Side B: October 15, 1989

Oh, goddamn. Life's simple pleasures! At least I'm not wearing diapers like some of my buddies. Okay, where was I? Yeah,
that's right. So we all start having a nice little conversation.
Sarah's asking a lot of questions, mostly directed to Alfonso,
and we answer them. She's real curious about our circumstances, you know. Money, women, stuff like that. And we
talk and talk the whole evening. And then we both walk
Sarah—can't bring ourselves to call her Tootsie—to the little
boarding house she lived at. Women only. Nice place. She says
before we leave her that she cooked at this little café called
Hanson's down on the main street and that they served up a
real good Sunday breakfast. Said we should come by that
weekend and that we'd not be disappointed. Well, goddamn,
we were there that Sunday, me mostly to keep things from getting awkward for Alfonso, which he appreciated. He'd done
the same for me.

Anyways, their courtship started then. And it only lasted a
month! They'd go on walks and Alfonso would buy her little
things. He didn't have much money, but he was thoughtful
about what he got her. And she smiled and patted his arm and
called him Al, which he thought was funny because it sounded so white, you know? Sometimes I'd tease him and call him
Al, too. During that time, he looked more relaxed than I'd
ever seen him before. What few creases he had on his forehead
melted away like butter in a hot skillet whenever Sarah was
around. Anyways, it all went pretty well so I wasn't too surprised when they decided to tie the knot. They married in a
civil ceremony—Sarah hated churches and Alfonso was not
such a religious man—and then moved into a larger boarding
house that took couples. Alfonso started working both the
farm and any other side job he could find. He got goddamn
respectable! But they seemed so happy. I couldn't complain if
I saw less and less of him. He was a family man now.

Well, things got a little strange after a bit. See, Sarah got pregnant right away, which made Alfonso real proud. But she started showing real early. Too early. And Alfonso got a little quiet, real lost in his thoughts, you know. He'd not hear whatever I was saying. But, eventually, when Sarah's belly was sticking out almost to Nevada, Alfonso seemed to accept things. After all, she was beautiful and good to him. Things could be worse. So Sarah goes into labor one night in January 1928 during the off season, so Alfonso was home a lot. I'll never forget that night. I was having a drink at the Tin Roof and Alfonso comes in looking pale. His hands shook and he was soaked through with sweat. He wore no jacket, just a thick shirt, and I yell at him that he's going to get pneumonia or something. He walks up to the bar and asks for a brandy and he just stares straight ahead. When his drink came, he throws it back and asks for another. He was making this strange little squeaking sound with his mouth. His teeth, I guess.

"Hombre," I says. "¿Qué pasa?"

He throws back the second shot and asks for another. After finishing the third, he says, "The baby was born tonight."

I smile and hit him on the back. "Wonderful!" I yell. "You're a papa!" But he's not smiling. "What's wrong?" I ask.

And he tells me. Slowly at first. It was a horrible story. Are you sure you want this for your report, Patrick? Okay. Here goes.

When he came home that night from working at McPheeter's ranch with the horses, Sarah was already in labor. This was seven months after they married. Anyways, she's in horrible pain and Alfonso says he wants to get someone to help but she screams, *"No!"* She says it's too late. He'd have to help her. Well, he realizes there's no way out so he goes and washes up and makes her as comfortable as possible. But she's in real pain and she's burning up with a fever and yelling weird things. That's when Alfonso first heard her scream out,

"Eurt!" He didn't know what she was saying. But he puts a wet cloth on her forehead and tries to calm her. She keeps on yelling, *"Eurt! Eurt! Eurt!"* And then she calms down suddenly and the baby comes without much warning at all. It turns out to be an easy delivery. Except for that one thing.

Alfonso described that baby to me real slow. A boy. Overall, handsome with lots of dark hair. Dark skin. Could've been Alfonso's. But one thing wrong. His right hand. He had only one finger, the index finger. The rest of his hand was smooth and narrowed down to the wrist. Looked kind of like a wriggling snake, Alfonso said. And when the baby moved that one finger, chills went down his back. He said that when he showed the baby to Sarah, she didn't react at all. Not a smile, not a scream. She just reached for him and put his little mouth on her breast. Alfonso stood there, bewildered, and then the baby started to play with Sarah's other breast with that snake of a hand and Sarah didn't mind a bit. That's when he said he had to go get things for the baby but, instead, came right here to talk to me.

What did I say to him? Well, what would you say? I lied. I said it didn't matter. Plenty of kids are born without body parts and that's just life. At least the baby had one good hand. Said Sarah was one beautiful and kind woman and he had more than most men. This little speech and the booze seemed to calm him down some. I told him that his wife and son needed him right then and that he should go home. He nodded slowly and had one more drink before leaving. But, despite my words of comfort, I felt sick. I knew something bad was going to happen. And, sad to say, I wasn't wrong.

As far as I know, they never baptized that baby. And Sarah insisted on naming him Eurt, that weird word she kept yelling when she went into labor. Alfonso couldn't deny his wife anything, so he agreed. Shit! What a name! Anyways, I tried to be a good friend and visited them as much as I could. But Eurt gave me the creeps. He was a handsome boy, but that hand and that stare! He'd stare at me like he was reading my thoughts. And he never smiled. I swear to God! I mean, *that* is not natural. You were a happy, smiling baby when my daughter brought you into this world nineteen years ago. Most babies are. But not this one. And Alfonso saw it, too. Only Sarah didn't seem to care. She cooed and sang to that baby like nothing was wrong. She loved that baby more than Alfonso, I'd say.

In March 1928, I was staying in the men's boarding house because it was the off season and I couldn't live in the camp. Had three or four odd jobs to keep me going until picking started again in a couple of months. One night, just before I went to sleep, Alfonso comes to visit. He looks sick. Pale, with deep purple circles under his eyes, hair matted and greasy.

I ask him, "What's wrong?"

And I can't believe his answer: "They're killing me. Slowly killing me."

What the hell did that mean? I thought. So I says, "Who's trying to kill you, Alfonso?"

And he looks at me with eyes going wild: "Sarah and Eurt. And I think it's Eurt's idea, too." Now, what could I think? Alfonso's gone off the deep end?

So I say, "Calm down, boy. No one's trying to kill you. What are they doing to you?"

And then he closes his eyes and I suddenly realize that he looks like a skeleton. He is so thin. Finally, after a few moments of silence, like he was listening to some voice, he says, "Poison. They're poisoning me."

"How?" I ask feeling more than a little shaky. "How?"

"The poison is everywhere. In my food, my drink, even in Sarah's kisses. And Eurt is behind it!"

Well, Patrick, I didn't know what to say except he certainly looked like he was moving from the land of the living pretty fast. I start to say something but he puts his hand on my shoulder, looks deep into my eyes and says, "I'll kill both of them before I let them kill me."

And I knew he meant it. So, crazy or not, what could I do? I had to think. So I says, "Alfonso, boy, I've been thinking of moving out of this town. Maybe go up to 'Frisco. Good jobs up there. And not so goddamned hot in the summer. Come with me. Okay, hombre?"

He looks at me for a minute. Just a minute. And he says, "Yes, I will. Let's go tonight."

Shit! I hadn't really planned on going up north but I figured I'd better go with the flow, as you kids say nowadays. Because, if I didn't, my friend would commit a double murder soon. So we packed. Yep. We had very little. Alfonso put a few dollars in a handkerchief and left it by the door of their boarding room. See, he still loved Sarah. He still had a heart. And then we left. We stole a couple of horses from the ranch Alfonso worked at and started north. We could've been strung up for stealing horses, but we had no choice, really.

After about an hour or two, we hear something awful strange. First, it starts as a low rumble. Couldn't figure what it was. Then it gets louder. And we turn to look over at the river, in the direction of St. Francis Dam. We could see the outline of the structure, designed and built by William Mulholland, you know. He was L.A.'s chief water engineer back then. Built that dam to hold two years' worth of water in case an earthquake split the aqueduct. So we think maybe this is an earthquake. But what we saw made us lose our ability to breathe at that moment. The dam starts to shift and break apart and crumble. The noise of the water—two years' worth, mind you—shakes our bodies and the horses, too. Then we see it. A wall of water, ten stories high going into the valley and some toward us. I yell, "Shit! Let's get out of here!" Alfonso just stared at the water and froze. I could see that he was thinking about Sarah. I yell again and he finally agrees and we make those horses run faster than they ever had before.

We rode until morning. About five hundred people died that night, though maybe more did because a lot of the migrant farm workers weren't accounted for. We learned later that the water washed away whole towns like Castaic and Piru and anything near the river. Sirens and phone calls tried to alert people to outrun the water. Some made it. Many did not. Three hours after the dam broke, the town of Santa Paula, which was pretty much evacuated, got hit, destroying three hundred homes. And Santa Paula was forty-two miles downstream from the dam! Saugus got hit so bad. Totally destroyed. Sad stories, too. Like the fact that forty-two children who attended the Saugus Elementary School were washed away. Anyways, the names of everyone who died, or at least everyone they could identify, were listed in all the California papers the next few days. Alfonso and I saw Sarah listed, or so we thought. A woman by the name of "Tootsie García" was there, listed on the front page of the *Los Angeles Times*. We don't know why they used her maiden name. Anyways, Eurt was not there. Maybe because he wasn't baptized so there was no record. And Alfonso didn't bother telling the authorities otherwise.

Well, you know the rest. Alfonso and I get up to 'Frisco, finally, and got pretty good work right away. He eventually married again. Nice woman. Not so pretty. But they had five kids and twelve grandkids. Me, I married your grandmother, Hanna, God bless her soul. Had my three kids and seven grandkids including you. Alfonso died ten years ago. His wife followed him a year later. Heart just stopped. Her name was Eleanor. A good, honest woman, that.

Anything else? Isn't that enough, Patrick? Well, let me think. Yes, I guess there was something else. About four years ago, I was watching the news on that TV. And there's this story about a preacher in Bakersfield. He has this huge following. People say he can heal. Everyone who was healed swore by this man. They showed him preaching. Good-looking fellow. Looked a lot like Alfonso. About sixty or so. Thick gray hair and a fine mustache. And I stared at him. Then he lifts up his left hand. It's a nice hand, long and well-manicured. Then he lifts the other. And my eyes almost burst from my head. The other hand was only a finger. Like a snake. Wriggling and pointing as he preached about hell and God's wrath. He used that hand to heal, they said. He went by the name of Veritas. Story ended and I just sat there for about ten minutes, not moving.

Well, Patrick. Good enough for your report? No, I don't have any explanations, and I'm afraid to even try to come up with some. Sometimes in life there aren't any. At least, none that you'd care to accept. You're young still. You'll see. Right now, while things are more black and white, I'd recommend that you just enjoy yourself. And I'll tell you one thing: wish I'd gone to college. Sounds like you're having some fun interviewing old farts like me. Want a Pepsi? Got plenty in the fridge. Okay, okay. Thought I'd be a good host. You are my favorite grandson, you know.

LA GUACA

here was a man who owned the finest restaurant in the pueblo. Though no name adorned the establishment, the villagers dubbed it La Guaca. The man, as well, had no name, at least none that the villagers knew. He was a complete mystery, a man apparently with no family, no origin, no history. So they called him El Huérfano.

One evening, as the villagers gorged themselves on enchiladas, tamales, pollo en mole, and other delectable dishes, El Huérfano rose from his usual seat at the corner table and cleared his throat. The room fell into silence.

"I plan to take a bride," said El Huérfano to the startled villagers. "But," he cautioned with a raised, elegant finger, "she must be perfect in every way."

Most of the families had at least one unmarried daughter because the Revolution had taken from this earth most of the pueblo's eligible young men. So this announcement raised great hope in the hearts of the parents and their hijas.

"I invite all of the pueblo's señoritas to feast here tomorrow night," said El Huérfano. "No one else may come. And I will choose my wife from among the guests."

"How will you choose?" an older woman asked. But El Huérfano turned and disappeared through a back door. A great cheer filled the void because this mysterious but wealthy man would make someone's perfect daughter a bride.

The next evening, all of the pueblo's single women swarmed La Guaca dressed in their finery. Though El Huérfano was not the handsomest of men, times were hard and there was little chance of living a comfortable life without a marriage of convenience. Remarkably, all of the women found seats in La Guaca and waited. The tables groaned with great platters of food and bottles of fine brandy. Finally, after what seemed an eternity, El Huérfano appeared.

"As you know," he began, "I am searching for the perfect wife."

The room murmured in anticipation.

"Before you sits a great feast," he continued, noticing one particular beauty who sat motionless amidst the others. "But it is poisoned."

A horrified gasp rose from the young women.

"The poison is so potent, it will kill in a matter of minutes." El Huérfano now whispered, "But it will not harm a perfect woman. If you wish to leave, please do. Otherwise, enjoy your dinner."

Only one woman stood and left. The others slowly served themselves and commenced eating, each believing that she would survive. After a few minutes, the first victim fell. And then there was another and yet another. Finally, only the most beautiful woman was left. She stood and walked to him.

"You shall be my wife," he said as he moved his lips to hers.

She leaned forward and they kissed. El Huérfano could taste the wonderful feast from the beauty's lips. But then his eyes bulged and he fell back.

"¡No!" he sputtered as he dropped to the floor.

"Sí, mi amor," said the beautiful woman. "Sí."

Don de la Cruz and the Devil of Malibu

on Jesús Reymundo de la Cruz slept with the Devil. No, this is both too euphemistic and inaccurate. Don de la Cruz screwed the Devil, fucked the Devil, but never slept with the Devil. La Diabla. As most of us know, the Devil who lived in Southern California was a female, so she was La Diabla, not El Diablo. Because the Devil is legion, the Devil resides in most towns and cities and may be a man or a woman. It all depends on what is needed. So in Southern California, the Devil is a woman. In New York, a male. Anyway, Don de la Cruz was La Diabla's sex mate and for that he gained great power and wealth as payment.

La Diabla lived in Malibu. But this is not the Malibu that you're imagining right now. No, she did not live in the Malibu of Johnny Carson, Olivia Newton-John, Gladstone's, and the Pacific Coast Highway that was used for the opening credits in the 1960s sitcom "Gidget" before Sally Field was the Flying Nun and Norma Rae and before everyone *really* loved her. No, this was the Malibu of 1822 long before any of that bullshit. But I'm getting ahead of myself. First, a little history. Because without history, stories cannot settle in a place that elucidates and adds shadows and meaning. And, as the Devil well knows, without a sense of history, holocausts are repeated and the Devil wins another battle.

If your fathers and mothers have not already taught you, forty-four poor Spanish settlers founded El Pueblo de Nuestra Señora la Reina de los Ángeles de la Porciúncula on September 4, 1791. The pueblo eventually became known simply as "Los

Angeles." The Spanish settlers converted to Catholicism the native Indians, known as the Tongva, who had already occupied the region for thousands of years. When Mexico severed its ties with Spain in 1822, Los Angeles became an important Mexican colony and would remain so until, twenty-four years later, the United States waged war on Mexico after gold was discovered in California. President James Polk called it Manifest Destiny. But that's a different story.

In 1822 Don de la Cruz was a wealthy man of thirty-two. For twelve years he had fucked La Diabla and, as I said earlier, she paid him well for his services. Don de la Cruz owned and operated the largest bank in El Pueblo de Nuestra Señora la Reina de los Ángeles de la Porciúncula. Through very little effort, he held one, two, sometimes three mortgages on most of the town's prime and not-so-prime properties. He lived in a thirty-room mansion built in the French style and ten servants met all his needs. Don de la Cruz dressed impeccably and looked handsome with a trim figure, white skin, and black hair. He said he was Spanish, not mestizo—not an ounce of pinche Indian blood ran through his veins, he said. When he walked the streets, people bowed and lowered their eyes and Don de la Cruz felt as important as a king.

But at the age of thirty-two, Don de la Cruz grew bored and weary of his success. Not that his success was not earned. Oh, no! Fucking La Diabla was a painful and ugly chore! She had a voracious appetite for him. Though La Diabla was as beautiful as any creature that walked this earth, her various orifices let out the rank stench of rape, mayhem, torture, and all things horrible and terrifying. And when Don de la Cruz inserted himself into La Diabla, a burning, gut-wrenching pain traveled up through his lower intestines, up into his stomach and toward his heart, where the pain wrapped itself like the clenched fist of a drowning man. And La Diabla would squeeze him with her beautiful thighs and scream such hideous screams that he had to grasp his ears, close his eyes, and put his mind someplace else far from this atrocity that he fucked.

All this happened in La Diabla's home under the rocks of Malibu in a cave—lined with the souls she had conquered—just out of sight of the wandering Chumash Indians, for they were the Malibu people, different from their relatives in town, the Tongva. And it was one day in April 1822 after fucking that Don de la Cruz lay by La Diabla and broached the subject of his boredom.

"I need a challenge," he began slowly, knowing that La Diabla had a horrible temper and reacted with lightning speed to anything resembling a threat to her power.

La Diabla turned to the man who lay near her in her bed of seaweed. "I'm not challenge enough?" she hissed.

"I mean," he continued, "my wealth and power within the town doesn't mean much to me anymore. It's too easy. Do you know what I mean?"

La Diabla smiled. Of course she knew what he meant. She had expected this day to come and so she had planned a response for his plea.

"In one month, you will have a challenge."

Don de la Cruz jumped. "What will it be?"

La Diabla smiled and grabbed her man's penis and squeezed until he almost screamed.

"You will know it when it presents itself to you," and with that, La Diabla mounted him and fucked him again. "And, in order to prepare you for that day, you will not share my bed between now and then. So, my love, fuck me so that I can remember what you feel like!"

After they were done, Don de la Cruz got dressed and went to his thirty-room mansion built in the French style with the ten servants who met all his needs and he waited for his challenge.

Throughout the month of April, he wondered who or what his challenge would be. A warrior, perhaps? A natural disaster? What, he wondered, did La Diabla have in mind?

As he thought and the days passed, Don de la Cruz noticed subtle changes in his town. Slowly, one by one, the landowners paid off their mortgages and withdrew their money from his bank. And, as he walked through the town, people no longer bowed and lowered their eyes as they had before, but instead they whispered, pointed, sneered, and showed no respect for the great Don de la Cruz. Finally, the greatest insult occurred: each and every one of his servants left his mansion. There was no one left. No one to cook for him, to dress him, to keep the horses brushed and fed, no one to care for his every need.

Don de la Cruz grew angrier and angrier and angrier. But he dared not go to La Diabla. He knew better. So he waited. The twenty-second day, the twenty-third, and finally the thirtieth day arrived on a sunny spring morning. He rose from bed, bathed, dressed, and cooked himself a big bowl of menudo— for he had taught himself to cook because he no longer had any servants! And he drank much brandy and waited.

At ten in the morning, he still sat at his dining table after finishing three bowls of the tripe and hominy soup and a whole bottle of brandy. And he sat and waited.

"¡Basta!" he finally yelled and shoved his bowl, glass, bottle, and candelabra onto the hard wood floor and stomped toward the front door of his mansion. He took a long breath from his narrow Spanish nostrils to prepare himself, grasped the large brass doorknob with his powerful pistol hand, and threw the door open. Don de la Cruz marched out of his mansion with all the resolve of his brave stallion, but suddenly he froze in mid-stride, in the dead center of his grand porch.

Standing before him was the entire population of the town. Just staring at him. All he could hear was their breathing, in unison, and not one bird or other creature dared make a sound. He stood on his porch, frozen for one full minute as his brandy-soaked brain tried hard to absorb what faced him at that moment.

And then he noticed her. A little girl, maybe thirteen or so, standing in the middle of the crowd. She looked like—no, I can't describe her—that would be impossible. But let me say that to Don de la Cruz she looked like everything that La Diabla was not. She wore a simple brown dress and her skin was brown as well, like the Indian that she surely was, and she wore no shoes. The girl carried a large wooden box and Don de la Cruz could see that carved on the box was an eagle with a serpent in its beak, and the eagle was perched on a cactus.

Ah! thought Don de la Cruz. Pistols! La Diabla has sent her challenge to me.

"Little girl," he said. "Are you my challenge with your box of pistols?"

The little girl said nothing but motioned to a man next to her and the man quickly brought a table and two chairs and put them between the girl and Don de la Cruz. She set the box on the table and opened it. And she said, "No pistols. Dominoes."

Don de la Cruz stood on the porch. He started to shake and the crowd murmured in confusion. And then he started to laugh. And he laughed with all the strength of his body. "Pinche dominoes!" he yelled. "That is my challenge!" And he laughed some more.

The crowd remained dead silent. And the girl threw down a challenge: "If I win, you will leave this town forever."

"And if I win, mija, what do I get?"

The girl smiled: "Whatever you want."

Don de la Cruz thought for but a moment and said, "¡Tú! I will have you and you know precisely what I mean, mija!"

The crowd let out a gasp, a sound of revulsion and fear.

"Yes," said the girl. "Yes, that is a bargain." And she sat down and poured the dominoes onto the table. They made a rattling sound like the sound when an old man dies and lets out his last breath.

Don de la Cruz walked slowly down the porch stairs, his beautiful black boots making a loud and majestic sound with each step. He sat down and said to another gasp of the crowd, "I can't wait to take you to my bed, mija."

The girl did not blush, nor did she betray fear. She simply said, "Choose your dominoes."

So the man and the girl chose their dominoes and each lined them up and examined their choices. "You may go first," said the little girl. And the crowd laughed.

"No!" yelled Don de la Cruz. "I will not be embarrassed by a pinche little Indian girl! You will go first."

The little girl shrugged a little shrug and complied. She put down a double six. Don de la Cruz's face turned as purple as a ripe fig, for as any child knows, the person who picks a double six always goes first. So! he thought, she was trying to humiliate me!

"¡Puta!" said Don de la Cruz through his perfectly aligned white teeth. "You will lose and you will be mine!"

But the game continued and lasted for two full days. Piece by piece, the pattern of dominoes grew into an angular snake with many eyes and the girl remained calm.

At one point, hours into the game, Don de la Cruz remarked, "Mija, you look familiar. Who are you? Do you live near our pueblo?"

"We have never met before," she said and put down a domino with a one and a five on it. "Never before."

Don de la Cruz shrugged and continued the game. It was now the first day of May and finally the little girl put down her last domino and there were no more to pick from the pile of dominoes that had once sat on the side of the table. Don de la Cruz's eyes widened. He felt ill. He was hungry and he had to piss and crap but he had not left his chair for two days. And now he had lost to a little bitch of an Indian girl! He grabbed the table and threw it to the ground, almost hitting the little girl's face with the edge of the table. The crowd held its breath.

She stood up and said: "I win. You lose. You know what to do!" The crowd drew near so Don de la Cruz decided not to pull his gun.

"Okay, mija. I may be many things, but I never cheat when I gamble. I have lost. And I will honor my part of the bargain." He went into his mansion and shut the door. The crowd stared at the door, hoping that Don de la Cruz would come out with a saddle and some food so that he could simply hop on his stallion and leave the town forever. Instead, he put a pistol into his mouth and blew the back of his head off. And as the crowd realized what had happened, a large roar of a cheer filled the air and the townspeople carried the little girl on their shoulders to the plaza to commence a wonderful fiesta that lasted two weeks.

And what happened to that little girl? Well, she eventually was given the honor of running Don de la Cruz's bank and grew wealthy and powerful and eventually held one, two, or maybe three mortgages on most of the town's prime and not-so-prime properties. She lived in Don de la Cruz's thirty-room mansion built in the French style with ten servants who met all her needs. She also dressed impeccably and looked beautiful with a trim figure, brown skin, and black hair. When she walked the streets, people bowed and lowered their eyes and she felt as important as a queen.

And she laughed to herself when she remembered how Don de la Cruz thought he remembered her. She did not lie. They had never met. But she looked familiar to Don de la Cruz because she was his daughter—the result of Don de la Cruz's many years of fucking La Diabla. She was born fully formed that month when the devil and her lover were separated.

La Diabla continues to run El Pueblo de Nuestra Señora la Reina de los Ángeles de la Porciúncula which today is simply known as "Los Angeles." And she still lives in Malibu. But not in the rocks by the ocean with all that seaweed. No. La Diabla submitted a building permit application with the California

Coastal Commission in 1986 so that she could build a luxurious house not far from Johnny Carson's beautiful home. The Coastal Commission granted her permit application, with a few conditions, but the house was eventually built and La Diabla enjoys life very much in Malibu on the beach.

Four Seasons

El verano

Inés yells *¡Chingao!* as her hand slips and the thick sewing needle slices through her left earlobe and into the cork faster than she wants. She could have said *Fuck!* but she hates the sound of that word because it's what her older brother, Jesusito, whispered in her nine-year-old ear as he fucked her for two years while their parents slept down the hall. He's gone from home now. Somewhere. Maybe dead. But his raspy *Fuck!* is still here. Still very much alive in his sister's head. So Inés yells *¡Chingao!* instead as her earlobe erupts and splatters blood across Julia Roberts' big white smile, making random crimson islands adrift in an ocean of gray newsprint. Inés should be in summer school right now: geometry, to be exact, but instead she needs to pierce her ears because she promised herself that she'd do it before she chickened out. Later, when her earlobes burn with fever and fill with yellow pus, her mother will ask, Why not just go to the mall and get it done? Inés will look down at her too-large feet and not answer, wondering why her mother hadn't had her only daughter's ears pierced as a baby like all good Mexicans. But Inés can't bring herself to ask such a logical question. I don't know, she says instead. *No sé.*

El otoño

Inés rode the bus with her friend Dolly. Dolly is Chinese and Dolly is really her given name. Her parents speak Mandarin, mostly, and thought that Dolly was a pretty American name. Now, they walk on Main Street toward Acapulco Gold, a new hangout that serves coffee and gourmet sandwiches to the young, artsy loft-livers. Inés could pass for eighteen, but Dolly looks very much her fourteen years. The artsy coffeehouse patrons like them and enjoy the company of these beautiful young girls who should be in school. Funny. Inés is more herself skipping school. Or so she thinks. They enter Acapulco Gold and the deep, rich smells of morning espresso, perfume, and cologne fill her nostrils and the happy chatter and hissing coffee machine envelope her, swathing her mind in thought-ending sounds. The walls are lined with miniature oil paintings of bullfighters, each in a different pose, all in bright yellows, reds, and greens punctuated by the broad black strokes of the bulls' straining muscles. Hey, says Duncan from behind the counter. Inés can barely discern a remix of an old Jackson Five song. Dolly is eyeing a boy by the magazines and because Inés has Duncan all to herself she answers, Hey. Duncan is an actor who hasn't acted for money yet. Inés likes his pale face, green eyes, carefully spiked blonde hair. The usual? he asks her. Inés settles onto a stool; Dolly is perusing the magazines. Yes, she says. The usual. Duncan's smile broadens. Coming up, he says. The usual for the pretty lady.

El invierno

Inés stares down at her mother's Nativity scene and laughs. The baby Jesus is about ten inches long and beautiful because he was made in Hungary of glistening white porcelain and is hand painted. He lies on his back smiling with outstretched delicate hands, his pink, dimpled knees bend a little, and he wears a fancy diaper or something that looks like a diaper. He rests in this wonderful little crib made of real wood with real straw for his mattress. Inés's mother sewed a little silk pillow for Jesus's head, just the right size. But the rest of the scene is made up of these cheap little plastic figures of the Three Wise Men and Joseph and Mary, all of whom are no more than four inches tall. And the little sheep and horses and cows are also small and made of cheap red and green plastic. There's even a little Rudolph with a bright red nose and a scarred Lassie that probably would be worth something if it weren't so beat up. It's all set up on the coffee table that is covered with flat, glittery cotton, like fancy snow. Inés just shakes her head at all of these little people and animals looking so cheap and plastic surrounding the beautiful baby Jesus, who looks very expensive and elegant. She shakes her head. Chingao, she whispers. Chingao.

La primavera

Inés keeps her eyes on the monarch butterfly that's resting on the other side of a dusty window. Its wings pump slowly, up and down, and the afternoon sun glides past it, through the open air of the loft, onto the polished hardwood floor. Duncan stirs, the sheets rustle, and Inés pulls in closer to Duncan's bare chest. The monarch's wings suddenly speed up, and it's gone, just like that, with a flash of orange and black, but Inés keeps her eyes on the spot where the butterfly had been. She likes the loft. Duncan's loft. Wide open. One big room. No school today. Her own holiday. Her fifteenth birthday. No one goes to school on their birthday. Right? Inés almost jumps. It's back! The monarch! Almost in the same place it had been. Inés smiles and wants to wake Duncan so he can see the beautiful butterfly. But she lets him sleep. He's so tired. So she stays quiet, still as a stone, watching the monarch fan its wings up and down. After a few minutes, she can no longer keep her eyes open. The rhythm of the butterfly's wings falls into perfect sync with Duncan's breathing. And, as she drifts off, unable to fight off two sleepless nights, Inés imagines that the monarch will be there waiting for her when she awakes.

You're the Only One Here

A thousand flying rhinoceroses happily winging their way over the Arco Towers toward Santa Monica? Yes, I guess *that* would be stranger than what's been happening to me. But not much. I mean, think about it: you know what a rhino looks like, right? Oh, yeah. You're an Animal Planet freak, so of course you know every permutation that thick gray wrinkles could offer. And you certainly know what wings look like. Now *those* can come in an infinite variety. Personally, I love the deep blacks and sunny oranges of the ruddy turnstone's wings. Their summer plumage, you know. You prefer a simple swan's? Figures. Elegant, graceful, white. Like you. Anyway if you put them together you get a flying rhino. What's so strange about that?

Dos

Pops used to say, "Uno nunca debe confiarse en la apariencias." You know, appearances are deceiving, or something like that. But not when it comes to me. I'm so ordinary looking. Pops always said that I was his beautiful baby girl, even after I graduated from USC law school. That's a father's love. He would never call me plain. But that's what I am. Plain and brown like a grocery bag. What? Oh, you're sweet. Thank you. I have little doubt that women love you. You know just what to say. Is it hot in here? I can play with the thermostat.

No, no. I'd better not open the window. The thermostat will do. By the way, are those handcuffs hurting much?

Tres

Well, it all started a few months ago. I was working away writing a draft opinion for Justice Bickerman. He loved my writing and usually didn't change a word. It was an interesting case involving a somewhat novel *habeas* issue. I remember when I finished the final draft, I set the neat stack of pages near my spineless yucca and dwarf silver nerve on the same table where my DeskJet sits, and I took a deep breath, feeling very proud. A few minutes later, I walked it over to Bickerman and he took it with a smile, the way he always did. I headed off to lunch with a grin on my face wider than a tasson spathiphyllum leaf. I almost skipped over to the Pollo Loco at the Grand Central Market a couple blocks from the state building. When I came back to my office, I found my opinion sitting on my chair. I did a little rumba to it expecting to see his usual *Fine job!!* written in neat red ink on the front page. Instead, a tiny, vicious scrawl said *See my notes.* So I opened it. He had massacred my work! Every page looked like a war zone with red slashes and Xs. My heart hit my throat with a thud. I turned on my heel and burst into his office without knocking. He looked so pathetic sitting there with a napkin tucked under his flabby chin, tuna on white and a Fresca sitting in front of him like pathetic sacrificial lambs. At first, Bickerman smiled. Then I threw my raped opinion on his food. Oh, you should have seen the fear drip into his eyes. But that's when it happened. I swear it did. I closed my eyes for but a second. I shut them hard with anger that went beyond anything I had ever felt before. When I opened them, Bickerman was gone. Pffffttttt!! Like that. You know it's true because it was all over the *Los Angeles Times*. Not all the facts. Only that he was missing and how his co-justices and poor wife couldn't imagine where he could be. Now, you have to admit, that's stranger than a thousand flying rhinoceroses. Right? Of course I'm right.

Cuatro

At first, I didn't think that I had anything to do with it. But it happened again, just three days later. I had this date with a guy I met after I was reassigned to a new justice in the other tower of the state building. What? James. A nice guy, or so I thought. He had worked as a research attorney for my new justice, but he was transferring to work for another. Change of pace, he said. But now I figured his justice had finally seen through him. Anyway, James and I kind of hit it off so we ended up going out to Westwood to see a movie. At least, that was the plan. When he picked me up in front of my apartment, we sat for a long while in his parked VW trying to decide what to see. I voted for something with a little action in it. Maybe Arnold or Bruce. I figured, his being a guy and all, he'd be happy. But no. James wanted to see a romantic comedy. One with Ashley Judd, for God's sake! I started getting really pissed. But he kept on saying how Ashley—that's what he called her, Ashley, not Ashley Judd, like he goddamn knew her or something—he kept on saying how she got great reviews for this latest movie and how she was kind of coming back after a few disappointing outings. His word. *Outings.* His voice went on and on and finally I closed my eyes and tried to shut him out. And then silence. Pure, beautiful silence. And James was gone. Just like Bickerman. You know about him, too, because that one made the local TV news a lot once it came out that James was actually being considered for a judgeship himself despite being only thirty-one years old. Boy wonder, it turns out. Harvard undergrad. Stanford law. All this despite being born to a poor single mom in Van Nuys. Oh, well. He still would have made a shitty judge. I guarantee it.

Cinco

Well, now it's pretty lonely. I hadn't realized that most of the people I socialized or worked with were such assholes. But they're all gone now. You're the only one here that I can talk to without getting royally pissed off, Robert. What? No. I said that I can't. I'm so alone. I need you here. I'll keep you fed and clean. Don't worry. No, I said. Robert, what part of "no" do you *not* understand? Stop it. Stop it! You don't realize how good you've got it! No! Robert, one last time. Shut up. Shut up, now.

THE HORNED TOAD

T here was a man who lived in a small Mexican fishing village with his wife and three children in a two-room wooden house not far from the shore. The man was not a fisherman like the others. Rather, he made the fishing nets that were used by the fishermen. He had long, delicate fingers that were put to good use tying the tiny knots of the nets that he made. His nets were the best in the village because they could withstand heavy catches and he earned a good living selling them to the fishermen. The man lived a quiet but loving life with his bride of ten years and his children ages one, three, and five.

The man's daily routine was set early on in his marriage and he veered from it only in emergencies such as when one of his children got sick or when a terrible storm blew into the village. Each morning, his wife served the man strong black coffee and two pieces of pan dulce. He would eat his sweet bread and drink his coffee at their too-crowded dining table while his children played more than they ate and his wife attended to her never-ending chore of cleaning. After eating, the man would kiss his wife and children, take his little bag with his lunch, and head off to his little shop that was about ten minutes away by foot. When he got to his shop, he would open all the windows and sit down to his work of making fishing nets.

The man had a view of the ocean from his little shop. To rest his eyes, he would look up from his work every so often and focus on the waves as they hit the sand. Sometimes he would be mesmerized by the waves and lose track of time.

After finishing a full day of making and selling nets, he would pack up his empty lunch bag and walk home to his family.

One day, the man sat in his shop, looked out the window, and saw a rowboat sitting on the sand. He had never seen it before and did not notice who had put it there. He put aside the net that he was working on and went out to inspect the boat.

It was a simple boat with both its oars set inside. There was no net or any personal belongings in it and no name on its side. The man looked around and saw no one. The sun shown brilliantly as it hung at its highest point and even made the man's dark mestizo skin burn hot. He looked out to the ocean and saw the little island the people called El Lagarto Cornudo, which means "the horned toad." It was called that not because horned toads populated the island but because its silhouette resembled a horned toad.

The man often wondered what was on El Lagarto Cornudo. He had heard that getting there was very difficult because of the crosscurrents that had to be navigated. He thought for a moment about his wife and three children and his little shop. The man then turned and walked back to his shop, retrieved his lunch, and walked back to the rowboat. He looked around again and, without hesitation, pushed the boat to the edge of the water, got in, and started rowing in the direction of El Lagarto Cornudo.

The man enjoyed the broad movements of his arms as he rowed. It was in contrast to the delicate work he did each day making fishing nets. He breathed deeply the ocean smell. Rowing was easy and pleasing without any fight from the notorious crosscurrents he had heard about. Several white egrets flew by the boat and landed in the water nearby. The man rowed with his back to the island and the egrets stayed alongside the boat, hoping the man would throw them some bread. The man looked over his shoulder and saw El Lagarto Cornudo in the distance.

After a half hour of rowing, the man stopped to eat. He opened his bag and pulled out a tortilla filled with grilled fish and ate it slowly, enjoying the feel of the tender flesh in his mouth. The man then opened his bottle of red wine and drank deeply. He wiped his mouth and put the bottle away in his bag and started to row again. The island was much farther than he had realized.

Eventually, the man grew tired because he had entered the crosscurrents that made it harder to row. Suddenly, without warning, the boat jerked and started to twirl and spin and the oars flew in every direction. The egrets flew away helter-skelter. The man tried to stay calm and attempted to gain control over the oars, but to no avail. Every few seconds as the boat went around and around, the man could see El Lagarto Cornudo which, by now, was only about a hundred yards away. But he could not calm the boat and one of the oars flew up and hit him hard on his forehead and he fell to the bottom of the boat.

The man felt himself slip from this world into the next. His soul left his body and stood over the still figure lying on the bottom of the boat. The man looked so small to himself. The water became calm and the boat was eventually still. The egrets flew back and landed by the boat. The man's soul looked at the island. With one movement of his outstretched arms, the man's soul rose into the air. He aimed himself toward the island and flew around it. It was a beautiful island with many trees and plants and waterfalls. The sand of its beaches gleamed a white different from the darker sand of the mainland.

After surveying El Lagarto Cornudo, the man turned to the mainland and passed over the little boat where his body lay. He then glided toward the shore and over his little shop and eventually he found his little house.

The man entered a window of his house and found his wife working in the kitchen. She could not see him but looked up momentarily when he came close to her. The man noticed that she was indeed quite beautiful and had lovely brown skin and gleaming black hair. He used to notice such things, but with time he had forgotten how to look at her.

The man then went out the back door and entered the yard where his children would be playing. And they were there, as he anticipated, playing loudly and joyously. He watched them move and yell and laugh and his heart filled with a love that would have made him cry but he was a spirit, so he could not cry. The man looked up into the sky and before he knew it, he was floating again over the little house and headed back to the boat.

In a while, he was again over the boat and he looked down upon his still body. Without warning, the man started to fall fast and silently. All went dark.

"Mateo," said a voice. "Are you all right?"

The man opened his eyes. He lay at the bottom of the boat that now sat on the shore. Several fishermen looked down on him.

"Did you try to go to El Lagarto Cornudo by yourself?" asked one of the fishermen.

"What a dangerous thing to do with such a small boat!" said another.

The man rubbed his forehead and realized that he was not dead but very much alive. He thanked the fishermen and after gaining his strength, walked home. It was almost sunset.

The man entered his little house and saw his wife. She said hello and they gave each other a little kiss. His wife noticed the bruise on her husband's forehead but said nothing. His children came in and ran to him and hugged him. That night, they had a very good dinner of fish, vegetables, and bread.

The next morning, the man's wife served the man strong black coffee and two pieces of pan dulce. He ate the sweet bread and drank the coffee at their too-crowded dining table while his children played more than they ate and his wife attended to her never-ending chore of cleaning. After eating, the man kissed his wife and children and took his little bag with his lunch and headed off to his little shop that was about ten minutes away by foot. When he got to his shop, he opened all the windows and sat down to his work of making fishing nets.

After an hour or so, the man looked out his window and saw the same little rowboat that he had seen the day before. He set his work aside, grabbed his lunch bag, and walked to the boat. The man looked around and saw no one. He put his lunch bag in the boat and pushed it to the edge of the water. He looked around again and, without hesitation, pushed the boat into the water, got in and then started to row in the direction of El Lagarto Cornudo.

Several white egrets flew by the boat and landed in the water nearby. The man rowed with his back to the island and the egrets stayed alongside the boat, hoping the man would throw them some bread. The man looked over his shoulder and saw El Lagarto Cornudo in the distance. The sun was hot and he smiled as he rowed toward the island.

SEÑOR SÁNCHEZ

eñor Sánchez lived a rather nice life in our little pueblo of Dos Cuentos. He sat most days in the plaza by the statue of our pueblo's founder, Don Antonio Segoviano, and waited, eyes closed, lips pursed in a constant little hum, with his dog Chucho panting by his side. You see, people came to him to hear him talk. They paid a few pesos, dropping them noisily into an empty Maxwell House tin that sat between Señor Sánchez and Chucho. With each clank of the heavy coins, Chucho's ratty little ears would pop up, frisky and alert, and Señor Sánchez would smile as he leaned back into the weather-beaten fold-out chair. He held his elegant, unusually small hands draped over the brass head of his cane, and laughed with the same question: "What is it you want to hear?"

And the customers would tell him.

"A sad story," said Señora Cruz, a widow for these last ten years.

"A very funny joke," offered our priest, Padre Olivares. And he tipped his shaggy head toward Señor Sánchez. "One I can tell in my sermon next Sunday," he smiled.

"Will I ever find a wife?" asked poor fat Simón, the carpenter.

One day, the mayor visited Señor Sánchez. I sat not far away, at the Bar Americano, drinking my usual lunch of two (or perhaps three) bottles of Tecate beer, and listened to what the great man wanted. No noise came from the Maxwell House tin: the mayor dropped a nice fat wad of paper bills into the till. The sun hit my face, hard and true, and I put my cool bottle down with a little clink and waited for Señor Sánchez to ask his usual question. But he did not. What did he do? He smiled. That was all. And Chucho slept. The mayor stood, frozen, for a moment or two. And then he spoke.

"Speak to me as my son would," he said. "If he were still alive."

My heart beat hard in my throat. The whole pueblo knew of the horrible tragedy of Mario's death in April, three months earlier. It had rained so hard for six days. No one had ventured out. Finally, on a Sunday, in the afternoon on the sixth day, the sun peeked out from behind the dark clouds. Some of us went out to inspect the roads and it was there that we found him, head deep in muddy water by the side of Calle Verdad. Mario's body was so bloated that we assumed he had been dead for several days. And, of course, it was clearly an accident. The mayor fell into a dark sadness at the loss of his only child.

So, on that day when the mayor went to Señor Sánchez, I tried to listen. He smiled at the mayor and then I saw his lips move slowly. I strained and strained but could not discern a word. Señor Sánchez's thin, almost blue lips stopped as fast as they had started. The mayor jumped back as if a large, brutal man had struck him in the chest. And for a moment, the birds did not sing and the wind did not blow. I glanced at my watch and noted that the mayor did not move for a full three minutes! Finally, the mayor straightened himself, brushed off nonexistent dust from his fine blue suit, bowed slowly and elegantly, and turned on his heel. Within a few seconds, he was out of view.

The odd thing was what happened afterwards. When the mayor left the plaza, Señor Sánchez sighed and shook his head. Slowly he stood, folded his chair, patted Chucho's head, and wandered off. Chucho, for some odd reason, stayed put. As he walked away, Señor Sánchez turned, ever so slowly, and caught my eye. In my embarrassment, I waved and then turned to my newspaper. He disappeared within a few moments.

Señor Sánchez never came to the plaza after that. A month later, we learned that he had died in his bed. Padre Olivares said that he lived to be one hundred twenty-five, according to the church's baptism records. And, according to some of the older citizens, Señor Sánchez had been talking in the plaza since he was twenty years old. That is a long time to be speaking. No?

THE FOX

A woman lived at the far end of a peninsula in a modest adobe hut and she appeared to be quite happy living all alone. The woman was no older than twenty, sturdily built, dark like the other Indians and mestizos who inhabited that end of the peninsula, and by the standards of the time, very handsome. She had all she needed to live comfortably. The woman owned one goat that gave a great deal of rich milk. Furthermore, fruit trees grew all around her hut so that she never wanted for juicy purple figs, sweet, crisp apples, and tangy, fragrant lemons. Though many colorful birds and energetic rabbits lived amongst the trees and shrubs, the woman did not have the heart to kill anything. So she lived on fruit as well as on goat milk which, by her skillful hands, she made into rich cheese and butter. All in all, the woman's world was as complete and serene as she ever could have wished and she seldom had to enter town for her needs.

The people who lived at the other end of the peninsula viewed the woman with great suspicion because she needed no one else to make her happy.

"Who does she think she is?" they grumbled.

And some said, "She will learn someday that she needs more than herself to live in this world!"

Still others wondered, "How could she not want to mingle with us? Are we not good people? Do we not offer warm company?"

They were not so simple as to imply that the woman was a "bruja"—a witch—or that she had some alliance with a

67

darker power. No, the people on the end of the peninsula were not stupid. Quite simply, they let jealousy do their thinking. And their jealousy led to griping about the woman. Other than this griping, however, the people left the woman to her own method of living.

To the north of the woman's hut was a small but plentiful pool of fresh water that ran down the nearby mountain that the people of the peninsula dubbed "El Zorro," which means "The Fox." The water tasted sweet and all the people of the peninsula drew water from it for their daily needs. It was on these trips to the pool that the people saw the woman working around her hut tending her goat and making butter and cheese. The people stared at her, but she simply went about her business, singing a cheerful song in her native Indian tongue rather than in Spanish. This, of course, merely angered the people even more.

The water that ran down from El Zorro into the pool made a constant rushing sound that was loud though pleasant. Indeed, the sound encouraged the woman to do her chores at a steady pace and it helped the woman sleep soundly each night. One morning, after being lulled into a deep sleep by the water rushing down the mountain and into the pool, the woman awoke and, as was her daily custom, she went to feed her goat. She took a few steps to the small wooden table at the other end of her hut and pulled from beneath it a burlap sack filled with grain. The woman picked up a battered though functional bowl made from a gourd and filled the bowl with grain. She pushed the bag back to its place and headed to the door while humming a pleasant and ancient melody. As the woman attempted to step out of her hut, her feet struck something soft though substantial. She looked down and her eyes widened. A sudden shock of horror ran throughout her limbs, making her drop the goat's food. Before her, at the entrance of her little hut, lay her goat, slit from its throat down to its belly. The goat was drained of its blood, which made a sea of red interrupted only by the soft white of the goat's rich, thick milk that swirled within but did not mix with the blood. The woman jumped over the goat, ran to the pool of water, and threw herself on the ground by the pool's edge.

Where does such cruelty come from? she thought. She lay there for hours not knowing what to do or what else to think. The people from the other end of the peninsula saw her as they came to draw their daily water. They looked at the carcass of the goat and back at the woman and just shook their heads, saying nothing to her.

When the woman finally pulled her emotions and thoughts together, it was almost midday. She realized what she had to do but this realization only made her feel ill. The woman knew that she had to get another goat but, to do so, she had to go to town and barter for one because wild goats no longer roamed freely on the peninsula or on El Zorro. She stood up and went to her hut, turning her eyes up to the sky so as not to see her slain goat. The woman retrieved from a shelf some of her finest cheeses and put them into a large cloth sack. She then pulled a tin box from under her bed and gathered into her small but strong hand ten pesos. That tin box had once been filled with many pesos but over that last five years, since the death of the woman's mother, the little treasure had slowly shrunk. But it was a necessary withdrawal. Prepared to barter, the woman left her hut, carefully avoiding the sight of her slain goat, and headed to town.

As she entered the main street of the town, she kept her eyes ahead of her to avoid the stares of the people. They muttered, "Look, she needs us now." But they did not interfere with the woman's mission. The woman remembered how, long ago, her mother took her to town to buy the goat that now lay dead by her hut. The goat seller had a small adobe structure with a large fenced-off yard where he kept his goats. The woman remembered that it was near the end of the main street of the town, off a little street called Calle de las Máscaras. She remembered the name of the street because, as a young girl, she wondered why you could not buy a mask from the goat seller when, after all, the goat seller's adobe sat on the Street of the Masks. She also remembered that the goat seller was quite old and smelled of dirty leather and grinned a foul grin at her. But she enjoyed the memory of that day because she had been with her mother and she was allowed to choose which goat they were going to barter for.

By and by, the woman arrived at the goat seller's adobe and approached its large wooden double doors. The woman could hear goats bleating and their pungent but not unpleasant fresh dung-smell reminded her of her slain goat. She lifted the large iron knocker and let it drop with a solid pound and waited for a response. The woman looked to the left and then to the right and noticed that some of the townspeople slowed their pace as they passed the adobe. She heard muttering and clicking tongues that she tried her best to ignore. Within a minute or so, she heard footsteps, light and energetic, advance on the other side of the doors. Not the footsteps of an old man, she thought. And she was right. For when the right door moved and its shadow revealed the person on the inside, the woman saw a young man, perhaps her age, with tousled black, curly hair and skin as smooth and white as the sand. The man smiled a smile that was crooked like a dead spider's leg, but otherwise he had the most handsome countenance the woman had ever seen.

After a moment, the woman said, "I would like to barter for a goat."

"I know," said the man to the woman's astonishment. "I have already heard of the tragedy. The townspeople who went for their daily water at the pool saw what had been done to your goat. Come in through my home and we can look for a replacement."

The man led the woman through his simple home toward a large door at the other end that led to the yard. As she walked, the woman observed each object in the two rooms through which they had to pass and noticed that the adobe was well kept but sparsely furnished with only a few chairs and a table or two. Not a thing adorned the walls except for several bookcases with shelves stacked with large beautiful books. She also noticed a large painting of the old goat seller that the woman remembered from long ago. The painting hung in an ornate gilded wooden frame. The old goat seller's eyes stared down on the woman as if lust filled his heart.

"Where is the old man?" she asked.

"My father," said the man, "has long since left this world. I now sell goats in his place."

The woman could not help but smile at this new knowledge. She liked this young man. Finally, they arrived at the large door at the end of the adobe and entered the yard. More than twenty goats gamboled up to the man and bleated a noisy hello. Dust filled the air as the goats' hooves kicked up in excitement.

"Which do you want?" said the man as he patted one of the goats.

The woman held up her bag of cheeses and the ten pesos and said, "What quality of goat can I barter with these?"

The man laughed. "No need to barter. Choose one that you like."

The woman grew angry. "I am not a pauper. I can pay for what I need." And she held up her cheeses and ten pesos even higher to make her point more emphatically.

Realizing that he had insulted the woman, the man said, "You are right. With what you have brought, you may have that goat," and he pointed to the largest animal in the yard.

The woman looked at the goat and then back at the man. "I will take this one," she said pointing to the smallest goat that her eyes could discern from among the noisy and rambunctious herd.

"It's a deal," said the young man, realizing that it was no use to argue with this strong-willed woman. "But on one condition," he added. "You must let me come and visit it each day because that one is my favorite."

The woman smiled and said, "Yes, it's a deal." She handed the man the sack of cheeses and put the ten pesos gently into his left hand. She then pulled a small rope from her belt, tied it to the little goat, and left through the gate at the end of the yard. The man smiled his crooked smile as he watched the woman leave leading her new little goat by the rope. One lonely cloud cleverly found its way to the vibrant sun and the goat yard suddenly grew dark. The man laughed and went back into his adobe.

So, as they agreed in their barter, the man visited the goat every day. And each day the woman asked the young man about his life and about the town. The townspeople gossiped and wondered if the old goat seller's son could actually bring this woman to her senses so that she would move to town as a new bride. After six months of the man's visits, they did indeed marry in a large, boisterous wedding at the town's large old church. The woman moved to the man's adobe, bringing her little goat with her.

At first, the man and woman lived a happy life full of laughter, love, and warmth. The goats sold well and eventually they added two more rooms to the adobe and put a little hut in the yard for the new maid to live in. The woman no longer made cheese and butter, so she had to go to town to buy such things. Over time, she began to mingle with the townspeople on her trips to the marketplace and they grew to enjoy the woman's company. The townspeople felt vindicated in their belief that the woman was now finally and truly a whole person except for one thing.

Despite a full year of sharing their wedding bed, the woman did not bear a child. The man was very patient at first. But in the second year of their marriage, he grew cold and slowly his anger replaced the love he once had for the woman. By the third year, anger permeated his every thought, movement, and prayer. The townspeople began to laugh behind his back and spread ugly gossip about him. The woman grew lonely as her husband stopped speaking to her. The man eventually stopped sleeping in their bed as well but instead slept on a bench in the yard with the goats.

The only joy left for the woman was her daily visit to the pool for water. She would see her little abandoned hut and remember the peaceful and full life she had once led caring for her goat and making cheese and butter from the goat's rich milk. She thought about her mother, who had taught her the Indian ways and songs and stories. The woman's joy vanished when she realized that she had to go back to town to her husband's house.

One morning, as she returned home from drawing water from the pool, she saw her husband in the yard speaking softly to their maid. Their bodies did not touch but she saw a familiarity between them that she recognized. The woman turned her head and went into the adobe.

In the fourth year of their marriage, the maid gave birth to a handsome boy with tousled black, curly hair. The townspeople gossiped and the maid became surly and refused to work. The woman grew even more silent and accepted her circumstances. The man gave up the charade and moved his things into the maid's hut.

One night in the fifth year of their marriage, the woman lay awake in her bed looking out her open window. The moon lit her bedroom with the light of twenty candles. The woman thought that she had been less lonely when she lived by herself under the shadow of El Zorro. While wrestling with this truth, she suddenly noticed that the light of the moon had dimmed and a dark figure of a man stood at the window. The woman remained still. She saw that the man wore a mask of a canine—a dog, a fox, or a wolf—she could not tell from the distance. The man slowly lifted his left leg over the windowsill and entered the room. She could hear his breath echo within the mask as he came close to the bed. The man lifted his right hand and revealed a long and shiny knife.

As the man put the knife into the woman's soft brown neck, the woman noticed that the mask was indeed that of a fox. And her mind fell back effortlessly to memories of the mountain called El Zorro and of the cool, sweet water that ran down the mountain and into the pool by the hut she had once lived in. And she noticed how exquisite red-brown paint shone on the mask's surface and shiny dabs of raven black glistened at the fox's eyes and nostrils. The woman listened calmly to her breath as it slowed.

And as the man slowly dug the knife deeper into the woman's neck and dragged it down toward her belly, he remembered how, long ago, the woman looked so beautiful and peaceful tending to her daily chores when she lived alone near El Zorro. The man also noticed how the knife in his hand felt remarkably similar to the way it felt the night he did the same to the woman's goat all those years ago.

SIGHT

I.

Alfredo sits across from his best friend, Alfredo, who goes by "Al." Alfredo looks down at the open package that sits on his antique mahogany dining table. "Best fucking birthday gift you'll ever get," says Al as he drinks from his bottle of San Miguel. "The best, mi amigo. No shit."

Alfredo stands and his chair makes a squeaking sound on the hardwood floor. He then, very carefully, reaches into the box and pulls out the gift. "Heavy," he whispers. "Heavier than it looks."

Al smiles. "Yes, hombre. Pinche heavy."

Alfredo lifts the gift, a pewter plate, large and muted in the afternoon sunlight that invades through the bay window. "Looks like a plate," he says.

"Uno nunca debe confiarse en las apariencias," says Al.

Alfredo holds the plate higher and the sunlight glints off its side. "Appearances are deceiving?" he asks.

"Perhaps."

"What do I do with it?" asks Alfredo.

Al laughs. "The question is: what will it do with you?"

II.

"Mi amor, what is this?" asks Himilce as she runs her index finger along the rim of the plate. It feels cool and smooth to her touch.

"A gift," says Alfredo. "From Al."

"Really?"

"Really."

"Since when did Al acquire taste?"

"Now, now. Be nice."

III.

Himilce bounds out of their bedroom wearing blue UCLA shorts and a little T-shirt that says "Phish." Alfredo looks up from his *Time* and admires her figure.

"Gym?"

"Yes, mi amor," she says. "How else can I keep you interested in me unless I have buns of steel?"

"Not fair," says Alfredo. "You're beautiful *and* brilliant. You make Johnny Cochran look wet behind the ears."

"Yeah, making a lousy 75K a year."

"More than I make."

"That's different," laughs Himilce. "You're a writer."

"Have a good workout."

"I will," she says as the heavy oak door groans open.

"I love you."

Himilce blows a kiss to Alfredo and leaves.

IV.

A half-hour after Himilce leaves for the gym, Alfredo hears a sound coming from the plate. It sits solidly in the middle of the dining table like a shrine. Alfredo walks over to it. He hears voices emanating from the plate's murky silver center.

"Oh, that feels good," he hears. It sounds like Himilce's voice. He looks into the plate and sees her lying on a massage table at her gym. She has no clothes on and lies on her stomach. A young woman in white shorts and matching T-shirt massages the back of Himilce's thighs. Her white hands look like reverse shadows on Himilce's cinnamon skin. Alfredo wants to blink but he cannot. He leans closer.

"How about this?" the young woman asks Himilce. She works her small, strong hands up deep into Himilce's buttocks and down toward her crotch. The young woman closes her eyes and bites her lower lip with straight white teeth.

"Mmmmmmm," is all Himilce says. "Mmmmmmmm."

The plate suddenly goes blank and the voices stop. Alfredo says, "Oh, shit."

V.

An hour later, Himilce comes home. She has showered and her ebony hair glistens with moisture.

"Hola, mi amor," she says.

Alfredo sits on the couch. His brow is furrowed deep with lines.

"Everything okay?" asks Himilce.

Alfredo sits silently. Then, as Himilce walks over to him, he asks, "Good workout?"

"Oh, yes, mi amor. I really needed it."

"Get a massage?"

Himilce almost jumps. She coughs and runs her fingers through her hair. "Why, yes. Before working out. A quick one."

Alfredo sighs. "Hope it felt good."

Himilce coughs again. "Yes, it did." She looks over to the dining room table. The plate is not there and the table looks as barren as a desert. "Where's the gift?"

Alfredo looks at her.

"Mi amor, what happened to the plate?"

"I decided that it didn't belong here anymore."

"What?"

"It just didn't belong."

Himilce shrugs. She kisses Alfredo on the forehead and heads toward the staircase.

"Gonna go on the Internet for awhile," she says.

Alfredo sits looking at the gleaming polished expanse of the dining room table.

"It just didn't belong," he finally says with a little laugh. "Just didn't belong."

BLACK BOX

So, he was pretty much alone, except for us. When he would visit, he was about thirty-five or maybe forty years old. It was hard to tell. He stood six feet even—I'm sure he's still tall but with an inch or two missing from age—and he was very skinny with long legs that ended at two large black shoes with thick soles. He always wore the same black shoes. And he always wore clean, ironed khakis with a shiny black belt and a white long-sleeved shirt. His dark skin was pulled hard and tight across his face and he always had a grin—or a grimace—showing his teeth, and his eyes squinted from the smoke from his cigarette. His nose slid down sharply and then curved under like a spatula and he kept his sparse, black hair neat and slicked back. His eyes glistened a blue-gray like my real metal *Gunsmoke* pistol. If it weren't for the mottled chocolate hue of his skin, he could've been confused for a Brit. And when I hugged him, my nostrils filled with a mixture of tobacco and Old Spice. He would pronounce my name with a heavy accent so that "Claudio" became special and faraway and ancient.

I called him "Uncle Tío," which Mom thought was absolutely the cutest thing ever said by a six-year-old. Because, as you know, "tío" means "uncle" in Spanish, so the name I gave him was redundant. Sort of like the La Brea Tar Pits west of the mid-Wilshire area near Hancock Park. You know, where they have a great collection of fossils excavated from the huge pool of bubbling tar that still gurgles as noxious gas is created from beneath and slowly emanates in the form of large and small domes that eventually pop under their own weight. "La

Brea" means "the tar," so when Pop would say that we were going to the La Brea Tar Pits, Lizzie, my older sister would say, "You mean we're going to the Tar Tar Pits?" Anyway, it sounded right, for some reason, so everyone in my family called him "Uncle Tío" even to his face and he smiled and showed very straight but stained yellow teeth and laughed a smoker's laugh. His name was actually José Flores Novas and before I dubbed him the redundant appellation "Uncle Tío," he was known as "Uncle Joe." Actually, he wasn't exactly an uncle in the strictest sense. He was related to us, somehow, on the Zendejas side of Mom's family. But I could never get a straight explanation as to his true lineage.

Uncle Tío would visit from time to time completely unannounced except for a phone call made a few minutes before he appeared at our doorstep. I often wondered how many times he called when we weren't home and if he kept on trying, calling from a phone booth a few blocks away, hoping that Pop would answer so that he could come by and give me and my two sisters presents and have a nice visit with Pop. He always had presents. As I said, he would arrive a few minutes after calling, carrying a large brown Safeway bag and smiling, knowing that I was dying from curiosity about what was in the bag for me. I would think, forget my sisters. They could wait. What was there for me?

At the time, I had no idea where Uncle Tío lived but I later learned from Mom that he had a little apartment in downtown L.A. about six miles from our house. So, he had to take the bus on Pico Boulevard and get off by the laundromat that we had to go to every so often when our dryer broke down and then walk down Ardmore Avenue to get to us. Back then, in the mid-1960s, the neighborhood was mostly Mexican immigrants or maybe, like my parents, the children of Mexican immigrants. Though these days, the area is mostly Central American and some of the Mexican old timers now call it "Little Managua" just to make the point. And in 1970, the L.A. City

Council put up a big sign off the 10 Freeway at the Normandie exit dubbing the neighborhood "Koreatown," which just kills my pop because he fought as a marine in the Korean Conflict. He enlisted at age eighteen to prove that he was as American as the next guy, and saw action and was decorated. So, you can see how living in a neighborhood called "Koreatown" drives him nuts, especially because most of the people in the area are Latino. Pop has a remarkable capacity to accept other people and all their differences, but he also knows stark irony when it knocks on the door and introduces itself.

Uncle Tío worked at a gas station for many years and earned a good wage. He came up from a small town in the Mexican state of Jalisco called Ocotlán when he was fifteen, all by himself, and settled in Los Angeles. Mom says he was married once but his wife left him.

"He wasn't a bad husband," Mom told me later. "He never hit her. Your Uncle Tío just had a few problems."

And I remember how he would show up with a bag and say, "¿Cómo estás, Claudio?" with a very thick voice and then, after a momentary hesitation just to rile me up, he would pull out a Tonka Truck or a Pancho Villa puppet from Olvera Street or a Bugs Bunny coloring book. Uncle Tío would hold the gift just out of my reach, smiling with a lit cigarette tucked in the side of his mouth and would—ever so slowly—lower it into my hands. He then gave me the bag to take to my sisters.

But I would wait around a bit—my sisters wouldn't be going anywhere soon anyway—and watch Uncle Tío say hello to Pop and sit down on our dark green vinyl couch and cross one of his long skinny legs over the other and ask for a cup of coffee. Pop would go to the kitchen and talk to Mom about the request. Mom always stayed in the kitchen when Uncle Tío came by. Anyway, Pop would eventually amble back— with the hardwood floors creaking beneath the worn linoleum—and give me a wink as I hid behind the couch. Pop would very slowly put the coffee into Uncle Tío's outstretched hand and then, after this well-rehearsed routine, the visit would begin.

I remember asking Mom many years later why she stayed in the kitchen during the visits.

"Oh, I don't know," she began. "I guess I really didn't have anything to add to the conversation." I eventually understood what she meant.

Anyway, the visit would begin and Uncle Tío would start speaking in Spanish. I didn't understand very much of what was said because he spoke so fast, but every so often I could pick up a word or two. "Gobierno"—government—was one of his favorite words. He would wave his long hands up and down and laugh a nervous little laugh and talk about the government. I remember watching his cigarette burn dangerously low and close to the long fingers of his left hand as he spoke, but he always knew to put it out in the big lemon-yellow ashtray that Pop had set on the coffee table next to him. But before he smashed it into a little ball at the bottom of the ashtray, he used it to light yet another cigarette. And then, after an hour of Uncle Tío talking and my Pop not saying much of anything except for an occasional "hmmm" and "claro" punctuated with a stiff nod, the visit was over and he would thank Pop so much for listening and leave with a smile.

Last year Mom told me that she got a letter from Uncle Tío.

"How is he?" I asked.

"Oh, wonderful. He's living in Mexico, in his old town. He rents a nice little house by the main boulevard. He gets Social Security checks forwarded to him and has enough to live on and he's very happy now."

"Now?" I asked. Mom has a way of getting to things pretty slowly.

"Well, mijo, Uncle Tío had a lot of problems when he lived in L.A." Her English is quite good, though she speaks with a slight accent.

"I know his wife left him soon after they got married," I said. I was intrigued but I could see that Mom wanted to tell me the truth slowly. She spoke very carefully.

"You know when he would visit your father and talk on end about the government?"

"Of course I remember. I loved the toys he would bring."

"Well, mijo, he was very generous. He loves all three of you so much. I give him credit that with all his problems he never forgot about you and your sisters."

Now I couldn't wait to hear what Mom had to say. I remember that it was hot out—I think it was August—but the house stayed cool with all the downstairs windows open so that the thin curtains blew up away from—or sucked tightly onto—the window screens with every cross-current. I'm sure the house was once magnificent with its vast rooms, curved staircase, and grand closets, but it was in great disrepair and already rasped with age when my parents bought it in 1962. The intervening thirty-seven years hadn't helped. Anyway, I finally asked: "What was wrong with Uncle Tío?"

Mom sat there on the same green couch that Uncle Tío used to sit on almost thirty years before, except it had been recovered several times and now had heavy, dark chestnut fabric covering it. Linoleum no longer covered each floor of the house. Now thick rust-colored wall-to-wall carpeting cloaked the living and dining rooms like the autumn leaves we seldom get in Los Angeles. And then she said, "He used to tell your father that the American government had put a black box into his head and was monitoring his thoughts. He said that if he smoked a lot, that would make it difficult for them to decipher his brain waves."

My God, I thought. Poor Uncle Tío was—or is—a classic schizophrenic. I shifted in my seat, trying to allow this new information settle in. "So," I asked. "How is he?"

"Like I said, he's living back in Mexico. He says that life is good and simple. Every day he wakes up, shaves and dresses, buys a paper, and drinks coffee with his friends at a café. That's all." Mom smoothed the front of her thick cotton dress—too thick for the weather—even though it looked fine. She didn't look into my eyes.

"What else?" I couldn't resist. I needed to know. I could read Mom's body language pretty well and I knew there was a little more to the story but that she was creeping up on it like a skilled hunter eyeing his prey.

"Nothing much. Just that your Uncle Tío says the government can't hear his thoughts anymore. That's all." Mom looked up to one of the windows as its peach-colored curtain was blown up with a *flap!* and just as suddenly sucked down cheek-to-cheek with the aging screen with a muffled *thwap!*

"And?" I wasn't going to let Mom off the hook. She had started this.

Mom sat there for about ten seconds in silence with her ample figure settled comfortably on the couch like a content and patient hen warming her eggs. Then she finished: "He says that he removed the black box from his head with a knife a few years ago. That explains why his thoughts aren't being monitored anymore."

I looked at Mom trying to find something—anything—in her expression, but her face revealed nothing but a slight smile. Suddenly, she stood up and said, "Oh, mijo, I forgot about the coffee. Do you want a cup?" And before I could answer, she had scurried out of the living room toward the kitchen.

BURIDAN'S ASS

Carlos stood, his back to the bay window, arms crossed, breath held still. "This is fucked," he said. "Simply and purely fucked."

"Get a hold of yourself, mi amor," said Gabriela. She sat in the brown leather recliner in the corner of Carlos's den, cigarette burning close to her fingers. "You can always run."

"Not from him," Carlos said. His arms popped up away from his ribs and he grabbed the back of his head as if it were about to explode, skull shattering to bits against his freshly painted walls. "He'll find me. You haven't seen him in action."

Gabriela took one deep drag from her Virginia Slims and dropped it into the moist dirt of the miniature potted palm. It sizzled and hissed before dying.

"Which one do I choose?" said Carlos, shooting a sharp glance at the sliver of white smoke rising gently from the potted palm. "Which one would you choose, if you had to?"

"Easy," said Gabriela. She stood and then strutted, swish-swish, strong thighs sliding under her silk dress, over to the coffee table. She stopped suddenly at the table's edge, put hands on hips, and cocked her head, left and then right. "I would choose this one," she said as she slowly lifted one hand from a hip, like pulling a large magnet from a manhole cover. Gabriela then pointed a long finger at a small blue box sitting on one side of the table across from a red one. "This one, of course."

"You'd choose eternal life over a lifetime of wealth?" said Carlos with a snicker.

"Well, if you have to choose only one, why not?" said Gabriela. "What's the big problem?" she laughed, snorting, as she returned her pointing hand to her hip.

"Shit!" said Carlos.

"He said you have to choose by six o'clock tonight."

"I know, I know."

"Or else lose both."

"I fucking know, OK?"

Gabriela shook her head. "Pinche pendejo," she said.

Carlos's head jerked up, eyes glistening. "No, you're the asshole because you don't realize how hard the choice is," he said.

Gabriela pivoted on a heel with a loud squeak on the hardwood floor. "Buridan's ass," she said as she walked away from the table. "Serves you right for what you've done to Sheila."

"Whose ass?" said Carlos. "What the fuck are you talking about?"

"Buridan's ass," she said again. Gabriela kept walking, *click, click, click,* away from Carlos. "Just a little something I learned in Philosophy 101 at UCLA," she laughed.

"What?" said Carlos. He took a step, hit his shin on the coffee table. "What?"

Gabriela left the room. Within a few moments, Carlos heard the front door open and then shut hard.

"Whose ass?" Carlos whispered. "Whose ass?"

The Plumed Serpent
of Los Angeles

I know your parents, being good Mexicans, taught you that although Columbus came from Italy, the Spanish crown commissioned his voyage to El Nuevo Mundo and so his three ships sailed under a Spanish flag. Then, a bit later, Spanish conquistadors and missionaries with names like Hernando Cortés and Friar Bartolomé de las Casas and Álvar Núñez Cabeza de Vaca came and, as that son-of-bitch Cromwell did to the Irish, they liberated the native people of their "barbarian" pagan beliefs and gave them Catholicism. Or so the Spanish conquistadors and missionaries thought. For, as we say in Spanish: "La zorra mudará los dientes mas no las mientes." A fox might lose its teeth, but not its nature. In other words, just because the Spanish banished the old Aztec gods so that the people had to worship in churches, they forgot to ask the gods if they wanted to leave. Therefore, because the Spanish forgot their manners, the old Aztec gods hung around and did what they could to make mischief in the lives of the mestizos—the new people of mixed Spanish and Indian blood—so that they would never forget who were the true ruling powers of the land.

The same is true in Ireland: the ancient gods still rumble through the night or pop up on a spring morning and cause mischief on that beautiful green island. I know this because, believe it or not, I have traveled throughout Ireland. When I was much younger, I hitchhiked through most of that wonderful island (I stayed in the south of Ireland because I was too nervous to deal with the shooting up north!) and on more than one occasion, I saw the mischief of the old Celtic gods. Little things, sometimes. Like when I was having beer at a pub in Galway on the western coast—a nice pint of Guinness—and I looked up at the wall by the dartboard and saw a painting. It was a typical painting of Ireland's patron saints: John Fitzgerald Kennedy, his brother Robert, and the pope. Well, just as I was staring at the painting, admiring its workmanship, in a blink, the painting changed! Now, instead of John Fitzgerald Kennedy, his brother Robert, and the pope, I saw, clear as day, John Fitzgerald Kennedy, his brother Robert, and *Muhammad Ali*! The greatest boxer who ever entered a ring! Float like a mariposa, sting like an abeja! I looked around the pub and no one else was looking and I wanted to yell "¡Chingao!" but I just stood there, mouth agape like a pinche pendejo, clenching my pint of Guinness. But there he was, clear as an Arizona morning, Muhammad Ali, the former Mr. Cassius Marcellas Clay, smiling that sly little smile of his and looking at me with that twinkle in his eyes that he used to have—before he got sick and started shaking—you know, when he used to appear on *The Mike Douglas Show*, and tease him something bad because it looked like he didn't know how to act around black folk. That magical transformation of the painting on that pub's wall in Galway, that, mis amigos, was the work of a pinche Irish god!

Well, the old Aztec gods are just as bad. No, worse! ¡Ay Dios mío! Don't get me wrong. They won't kill or anything. But their idea of a joke can sometimes include a little physical and emotional pain. And they don't care who their next victim is. So, when the Spanish came, the old gods went underground and hid during the daylight but, when it got dark, they came back up to play their tricks on the mestizos and Indians. But this is where my story begins: the most pissed off Aztec god was, who else? Quetzalcoatl. Just like Ali, he was simply the greatest, and he ruled the Aztecs and the Toltecs with an iron fist. His fame continued even into the twentieth century when D. H. Lawrence, one of my favorite writers—you know, he's buried in Taos, New Mexico—wrote a novel and called it *Quetzalcoatl*. But his publishers were worried that with such a strange title, the book wouldn't sell so they changed it to *The Plumed Serpent*. Because that's what Quetzalcoatl was: a snake with many beautiful feathers surrounding his face. Few would condemn me for saying that Quetzalcoatl was probably the greatest god the Americas have ever known.

Now, Quetzi—as his friends called him because, let's face it, even for gods, "Quetzalcoatl" is quite a mouthful—Quetzi was a grouchy son-of-a-bitch because, well, you would be too if you were a great god and then the Spanish told your people to worship Jesus Christ and they do—can you believe it!—they do. This Jesus, fumed Quetzi—doesn't require human sacrifices! Hell, he let *himself* be sacrificed! What kind of god does that? And then, to top it off, other people, pale people, come and take over the land he once ruled.

Now, most of the other Aztec gods took on human form the way you would if you were in their position. Gods with names like Huitzilopochtli, Chalchihuitlicue, and Tlacahuepan became José, María, and Hernán. They looked at the human population and found the best-looking examples of humanity they could. Sometimes they mixed and matched different features. But they chose good-looking hombres y damas and transmuted into these beautiful people! The best looking faces and legs and arms and man-oh-Manischewitz! They were the best-looking Mexicans you ever saw with skin as smooth and brown as polished Indian pottery with raven-black hair that glistened in the sun! And, at night, only at night, well after midnight, they changed back into their original forms and flew through Mexico and played their evil tricks on the poor unsuspecting Jesus-worshipping mestizos and Indians.

But Quetzi was so angry that he left Tenochtitlan—you know, Mexico City—and wandered without purpose for almost three hundred years. He eventually headed north until he found a little one-room hut far from his home in a place that would eventually be called El Pueblo de Nuestra Señora la Reina de los Ángeles de la Porciúncula, now known simply as "Los Angeles." You see, he had suffered greatly once before and this latest insult was too much for him to bear. It is a painful and embarrassing story, but you must know it to understand why Quetzi could not live in his home of Tenochtitlan anymore. Centuries before the Spanish came, the god Tezcatlipoca disguised himself as a great hairy spider and offered Quetzi his very first taste of pulque which—as I'm sure you know—is more dangerous than tequila. Oh! That shit will get you borracho! And Quetzi loved the feeling he got from the pulque and drank so much that, in a drunken heat, he had his way with his sister, Quetzalpetlatl! The *shame* of it! So, Quetzi banished himself and wandered the land for many generations.

But this Spanish conquest thing, that was too much for Quetzi to stomach. So, as I said, Quetzi left Tenochtitlan and eventually ended up in old Los Angeles living in a little adobe hut. And, in his disgust, instead of choosing a beautiful body to transmute into, Quetzi borrowed the looks of the first person he saw after the Spanish banned the Aztec religion. Unfortunately, the first person he laid his eyes on was a broken-down old borrachín who was bald as a mango with a large pot of a belly that hung below his belt. But Quetzi's anger blinded him so that he didn't care.

One day poor old Quetzi left his little adobe to look for something to eat. Yes, he now suffered from hunger of the human type. So he headed to the little hut owned by this vieja, an old Indian woman who bartered with anyone who wanted good Mexican comida and who had something she might want. But as he scrambled down some rocks to avoid taking the long way on the foot-worn dirt road, the stupid Aztec god tripped over his own feet and landed with a *thump!* right in the scrubby bushes. You see, the drunkard that Quetzi turned into had these goddamn big Godzilla-like feet, so it was easy to trip just walking.

Suddenly, as he lay there with a spinning head, Quetzi noticed a woman standing over him. A beautiful woman! And for a moment, his bitterness and grouchiness melted away and he felt a little joy in his rock of a heart.

"Quetzalcoatl?" the woman said.

Goddamn! Quetzi thought. This beautiful human knows my name!

"Quetzalcoatl?" the woman said again, this time with urgency in her voice. Before he could answer, the woman said, "We need you. We need you now!"

"Who?" said Quetzi, rubbing his nalgas as he stood up with the help of the beautiful woman.

"We do. The old Aztec gods. We need you!"

And at that moment, Quetzi recognized the beautiful woman's eyes. The rest of her face, he did not know, but he knew the eyes of his sister, Quetzalpetlatl, the one whom he had disgraced so many years before. He suddenly grew angry and growled, "Go to hell!" He dusted himself off and got onto the main dirt road. But she followed him.

"Please, O great Quetzalcoatl! Our way of life is being threatened and we need all the power of the old days to survive, to win! Please don't run from me!" The beautiful woman had great tears falling from her eyes as she almost ran by Quetzi's side.

Quetzi suddenly stopped and turned to the beautiful woman. His face burned a deep red and he sputtered, "Where were my compañeros when the Spanish came to banish us? Huh? Where?"

Quetzalpetlatl looked down, ashamed. Quetzi continued: "You did not fight then, did you? I asked you all to fight but you goddamn cowards just hid and let Jesus and Mary and Joseph and all those pinche saints replace us! You cowards! Leave me be! Do I look like a pendejo to you?" And with that, Quetzi started to walk with a quick gait, kicking up dust and rocks.

Quetzalpetlatl thought for a moment and, in a panic, she said, "If we win, you can rule all of us again! I promise!"

And, this, my friends, made Quetzi stop and think. Oh, to be the highest god again! Could he even remember how it felt? Quetzi looked out to the clear Los Angeles sky. He trained his eyes on a hawk circling in the eastern horizon.

Quetzalpetlatl saw that her brother was considering the possibilities. So to up the ante, she added, "And I will forgive you, and you will no longer carry shame in your heart."

Oh, joy! thought Quetzi. Can I have it all again? Is it possible? But it has to be done the right way. So Quetzi said, "Let's go and get some food, mi hermana, and talk about what is needed."

They found their way to the little hut owned by the old Indian woman to get something to eat. Quetzi's sister offered the vieja beautiful stones and, in exchange, received two wooden platters of pollo in a thick mole sauce and a large, steaming pile of corn tortillas wrapped in a moist towel. They then found a nice place to sit under a large pine tree so that Quetzi could learn what was afoot.

Quetzi's sister explained that the Christian god of evil, Satan, had decided to set up shop in the various cities and towns of the Americas. Satan, being legion, sent parts of himself throughout the land to lay the foundation for a revolution, to displace Jesus and rule the human race. But in order to topple Christianity, he also had to purge the land of the Aztec gods. A clean slate, he wanted. A complete coup. And the first place Satan was going to go was to El Pueblo de Nuestra Señora la Reina de los Ángeles de la Porciúncula. You see, Satan appreciated irony and what better place to begin than a pueblo named after Jesus's mother? As I told you, Satan is legion, so he sent the female part of himself, La Diabla, to plan the war against the old Aztec gods. La Diabla, it was learned, found a little cave in Malibu by the ocean and there she plotted.

"So," said Quetzi as he wiped mole from his round face with his already filthy sleeve, "all we have to do is kill La Diabla. Right?"

His sister thought for a moment and then said, "No, La Diabla cannot be killed. But she can be weakened. She can be taught a lesson. La Diabla can be seduced." As she said this last thing, she looked down and blushed a dark red-brown.

"Ah," said Quetzi, purposely ignoring his sister's embarrassment. "We must be clever." And then he laughed. "Why don't we pull that pulque trick Tezcatlipoca pulled on me all those years ago and get La Diabla muy borracha!" Quetzi let out a big laugh and then a loud fart, not caring because, after all, he had lived as an anchorite in his little hut for so long that his manners were atrocious.

"Perhaps," said Quetzalpetlatl, covering her nose as nonchalantly as possible. "But we must get you in shape first."

Quetzi looked down at himself and saw what she meant. He had chosen a poor example of a human form. But he felt needed again and said, "I'll do whatever you need me to do!"

So it began on that day. Quetzalpetlatl became her brother's own personal trainer. For two months, she made Quetzi run, eat small meals, lift large stones in the heat of the desert day, and stop drinking booze. And at the end of two months, Quetzi's belly had grown flat and strong, his face was burned a nice healthy brown, and his arms and legs had developed bands of pulsating muscles. And, my friends, while they were getting Quetzi in shape, they started to develop a plan, step by step, always trying to remember La Diabla's psychology.

In getting Quetzi in shape, his sister couldn't do anything about his bald head—he was a total pelón! But Quetzi allowed his beard to grow and his sister then trimmed it into a fine mustache and goatee. Quetzalpetlatl helped her brother find beautiful clothes to show off his new physique. She stood him in front of a mirror in his little hut and they both admired his new physical power. Poor Quetzalpetlatl felt ashamed because she admired her brother in all his manliness, but she shook herself from within and said, "You are now ready to seduce La Diabla and save us!"

As I've told you, La Diabla can't be killed, but her power can be limited, tied in knots. And she loves bargains. It's funny. La Diabla is vicious and evil but she always keeps a bargain. The trick, though, is to lure her into a bargain that will backfire and, to do that, you have to rely on her own failing: pride. Remember, pride led Satan to be cast from heaven in the first place. And as they say in America, you can't teach an old dog new tricks! So they hatched a plan whereby Quetzi would challenge La Diabla to a duel of sorts. A duel of gods. If La Diabla won, the Aztec gods would leave this world without protest. But if Quetzi prevailed, La Diabla would leave the Americas forever and use the rest of the world for her playground.

But first, Quetzi had to go to Malibu where La Diabla lived. His sister bargained for a great stallion and a fine saddle and Quetzi prepared for his twenty-six mile trek to the coast. When all was prepared, Quetzalpetlatl helped Quetzi mount the magnificent horse. She said, "I love you, my brother."

"And I you," said Quetzi proudly as he dug his spurs into the horse and headed west.

Now the Chumash Indians lived by the beach at that time and, indeed, they named it Umalido, which means "where the surf is loud" and eventually became "Malibu." As Quetzi came within a few miles of La Diabla's cave, the Chumash looked up from their daily lives and stared in amazement at the striking figure cut by the newly minted hero-to-be. As he neared La Diabla's home, Quetzi's nostrils filled with the stench of evil and his horse became skittish.

"There, there, my beauty," said Quetzi in a soothing voice as he patted his horse's muscular neck. "All will be well." The horse slowly calmed and continued its march toward the profane shelter. When they reached the mouth of the cave, Quetzi could see nothing but black, so he dismounted and pulled a lantern from the side of his saddle and lit it. Slowly, wary of the rocky ground, Quetzi entered the cave. He walked, one foot gently placed in front of the other, for almost an hour. What the hell am I doing? he thought. What will become of me? The darkness of the cave almost swallowed the flickering light of the lantern. What will become of me?

Suddenly, Quetzi stopped with a crunch of gravel under his shining boots. He sensed a presence, though no figure appeared.

"What took you so long?" said an unseen woman.

The skin on Quetzi's bald head danced with fear. He sucked in as much air as possible and said, "It is I, the great Quetzalcoatl! Come out so that I may see you, Diabla!" And only silence answered him. Oh, poor Quetzi! What had he gotten himself into? But no response came so he continued to walk deeper into the cave. After walking for about ten minutes he stopped and called out again, "It is I, the great Quetzalcoatl! Come out so that I may see you, Diabla!"

And this time, he got his wish. Without a sound, La Diabla appeared before Quetzi. I cannot describe her other than to say that Quetzi's eyes had never rested upon a creature more beautiful and seductive. He could not speak.

"O great Quetzalcoatl, please, come and share a drink with me. I am honored to be in the presence of such a great god." With that, a grand oak table appeared before Quetzi. The table groaned with great bottles of pulque, large baskets of fruit, a roast pig, and many other delicacies. Quetzi's eyes focused on the pulque and he grew frightened as he remembered how he was made a fool of by the god Tezcatlipoca, who had disguised himself as a spider and offered Quetzi his very first taste of alcohol. But his mouth watered as he remembered the feel of booze in his mouth and the wonderful burning sensation it made as it flowed down his throat and into his belly. Quetzi shook his head and closed his eyes for a moment to clear his mind of all temptation.

"No," said Quetzi in a strong voice. "I am here to offer you a bargain."

"No," said La Diabla. "You must accept my hospitality and only then will I hear you out."

So they sat down, Quetzi at one end of the table and La Diabla at the other. I am still a great god, he thought. I can hold my liquor. I will not fail to present my bargain. And so they ate and drank in silence, both keeping sharp eyes on each other. Finally, after an hour of this, La Diabla said, "So what is the purpose of this visit?" As she said this, she could see that Quetzi was getting loose with the pulque. La Diabla smiled a noxious smile and waited for a response.

That poor son-of-a-bitch Quetzi! He hadn't had a drink in two months and now the pulque softened his resolve and made him think corrupt thoughts as his eyes perused La Diabla's unblemished and enticing brown skin. He shook his head again and reminded himself of his noble mission. Quetzi cleared his throat of the phlegm that pulque tends to invite from most men's throats and said, "No, I'd rather hear from you first."

La Diabla continued to smile. "Well, O magnificent Quetzal-coatl, you no doubt have heard of my plan to rid this world of the old gods. Otherwise, why would you be here?"

"Go on," he said.

La Diabla leaned forward and began, "I am sickened by the puny efforts of your hermanos to maintain a presence in this land. They are beyond irrelevant and they do nothing more than cause a low level of nausea to permeate my very essence."

"If we are so little, why do you care?" Quetzi made a good point with this question and he rocked his head back and forth to show that he was still in command.

La Diabla leaned even closer to Quetzi and the oak table creaked. She hissed, "Because as long as the mestizos and Indians know you're still here—and they do know because of the stupid pranks you fallen gods do at night—I cannot fully rule."

Good answer, thought Quetzi. As La Diabla spoke, Quetzi allowed his eyes to drink further of her beauty. His heart beat strongly within his chest and his groin flushed with the warmth of lecherous blood. What could he do? Could he forsake his fellow gods and cut a bargain to save himself and perhaps bring himself a little closer to this beautiful creature? He kept still and let La Diabla continue.

"So, great Quetzalcoatl, I offer you a bargain: Do not stand in my way and, in exchange, you may have a role under my reign."

Quetzi thought for a moment. Since the conquistadors had come and banished the Aztec gods, he had lived less than a life. If he rejected La Diabla's offer and followed through with his plan to help his brothers and sisters, maybe he could rule again. And didn't he owe it to his sister after the way he had defiled her long ago? But what if he failed? This powerful dark deity of Christianity could destroy him. Maybe he could save himself and get a little power to enjoy life again! Quetzi looked into La Diabla's eyes. He could lose himself in those eyes! Screw the others! What did they ever do for him? They had never visited him before this whole mess started. Screw them and his sister!

"I accept your bargain!" And he drank up another large goblet of pulque.

La Diabla laughed and walked over to Quetzi and said, "Let us walk to the outside world and start!"

So they left the cave arm in arm and went to the shore on the sand and stood facing east. The smogless late summer sky gleamed a blue that no longer exists and cool wind from the ocean blew hard and clean. La Diabla touched Quetzi's sleeve and within a breath, they were standing in the Santa Ana Canyon by the northeastern desert. She lifted her hands to her mouth and screamed a mute scream and, at that very second, Quetzi saw the true power of this goddess. La Diabla emitted a hot and relentless wind that began as a mere breeze but then erupted into a torrent of withering heat. La Diabla blew and blew and blew for precisely three hours and Quetzi stood there without the power to move, for he was in awe.

The too-beautiful Mexicans who were once great Aztec gods could not withstand La Diabla's wind. They withered and eventually their human forms died within those three hours. Their souls rose up and went to a place beyond the moon far from their earthly home. La Diabla was now supreme!

La Diabla kept her bargain with our friend Quetzi. She let him live different lives throughout the centuries to bring his own brand of misery to the human race. First, he began as a banker, then a governor, lawyer, movie producer, editor, mass murderer, literary agent, plumber, and right now, as I speak, he is the owner of a major league baseball team. However, Quetzi never got very close to La Diabla. But his dating life was full and, so far, Quetzi has walked down the aisle at least a dozen times.

And our friend La Diabla is doing her best to strangle our world in her own way. But because of her paranoia, and despite killing all the old gods except Quetzi, she still blows the Santa Ana Winds—the devil winds, as we call them today—to make certain that the former great gods of the Aztecs will never rise again.

Is there a moral to this story? No, not really. But there is an old Mexican dicho that applies: "Si se muere el perro, se acaba la rabia." If the dog dies, the rabies will be gone. But, mis amigos, I promise you this: The dog is not dead. She is alive and well in a little town called El Pueblo de Nuestra Señora la Reina de los Ángeles de la Porciúncula.

My Dinner with
Siskel and Ebert

I sit on a concrete bench that curves in a semi-circle around a cylindrical concrete table. Smooth, shiny pebbles adorn the tabletop like so many fish eyes. The man-made stone is cold beneath my buttocks; a chill sneaks through my well-worn corduroy trousers like a burglar happily finding an unlocked door. The bench and table crouch within a large two-walled structure with a decrepit bamboo roof. The traffic-filled Pacific Coast Highway hums to my left and the bleached sand nuzzles the blue-green water to my right.

A large paper plate of frijoles, arroz, and pollo sits before me. Near the plate, a pile of steaming corn tortillas is wrapped like a sleeping baby in a moist white towel. A glistening bottle of Dos Equis beer watches over it all. The sun sets, making brilliant red, purple, and yellow streaks through the smog.

Across from me sit Gene Siskel and Roger Ebert. They are dressed just as they used to be on their TV show. Ebert rubs his soft, round belly as he eyes his plate spilling over with chicken fried steak, French fries, and potato salad. In contrast, Siskel only has a small mixed salad and caffeine-free Diet Coke set before him.

Ebert suddenly shifts his eyes to my plate. Through large glasses, his eyes glisten like silver-blue sardines. Licking his lips, he says, "I should have ordered what you got."

I look at him with reproach and say, "Mr. Ebert, or Siskel, or whatever . . ."

Ebert knows my dilemma and says, "Ah! You can remember which one is which with a little trick. 'Siskel' begins with an 'S' and so does the word 'skinny.' So I'm Ebert."

"Thank you," I say. "So, Mr. Ebert," I continue. "You really should watch what you eat. You're quite obese and you're very likely going to die way before your time like John Candy or that big guy from *Saturday Night Live*."

Ebert shifts in his seat and emits a low growling sound. Finally he spits out, "Does it really matter? I mean, look at poor Gene here." As he says this, he points his short, round thumb in Siskel's direction. "He always ate carefully and he beat me to the grave."

After Ebert says this, Siskel's small smile disappears and I feel ashamed to be sitting there. Siskel looks over at Ebert and, ever so slowly, starts to fade. Soon all we see are his sad eyes. After a minute, there is nothing left of him. A breeze blows hard through our little enclave.

I look at Ebert and he looks at me. His jowl-laden face betrays no emotion but he emits a little sound that is a cross between a whistle and a whine. The last remaining sunlight hits Ebert's face and transforms his wet lips into luminous, frightening things. Finally, he says, "Do you think Gene would mind if I ate his salad?"

I wake up before I can answer.

ON THE HILL

On the hill Arturo's house had stood for threescore years. In that time, he had married Eleazar, become a fitful though thoughtful father of two boys and one girl, watched his wife wither into nothing from a disease the doctors could not name or cure, and been left alone when his children abandoned Mexico for California and Texas in search of riches. Arturo's heart hung hard and heavy in his chest as he wandered his empty house at night, candle in hand because he no longer paid his utility bills—listening to the silence and watching the ghosts jump and roll and play. Dios sabe lo que hace, Arturo used to think. But now, as the empty house creaked and the candle flickered in the draft, he could not believe that God had known what he was doing when he took everything away from Arturo.

On the hill Arturo's house had stood for threescore years. The other villagers had lost all curiosity and concern for him long ago, and he appreciated living an unobserved life. He cobbled together his meager, solitary existence clinging to the essential truth of this dicho Mexicano: Más vale no ponerse en el tocadero. One should not place oneself in harm's way. So he grew his food, kept his chickens, and nurtured his two goats, thus relieving himself of the villagers' company.

On the hill Arturo's house had stood for threescore years. When the villagers found the chickens and goats starving, and the little garden dried up and crumbling in the wind, they ventured into the house. They found Arturo's body lying cold and pale with stench beginning, on his bed, curled in a ball, clutching the pillow that Eleazar's head had once slept on. The villagers said, "Vida sin amigos, muerte sin testigos." A life without friends, a death without witnesses. And Arturo's ghost laughed at the villagers' ignorance.

A MELANCHOLY CHIME

Part Six

A pig," she said.

Gabriel lay on his side, resting his head on his left hand while his thin legs spread out on the blanket like the Tigris and Euphrates Rivers. He watched Elisa's lips become a ripe, succulent plum as she pronounced the P in the word "pig." Gabriel wished she would say it again so he remained silent, letting the relaxing and constant sound of the Thames fill the void. The moonlight found its way just enough through the trees so that Gabriel could discern the fine features of her face and the deep color of her lips. His glass of Cabernet sat on the picnic basket and he reached over for it. The cool evening air mixed with the nice buzz of the alcohol and Gabriel felt alert and in control.

Elisa stood up and stumbled a little with her left foot catching the edge of the blanket. The dried leaves crunched as she found her footing. "He was nothing but a pig," she said.

Gabriel smiled at his little victory and took a sip of wine in a silent toast to himself. "Ah," he finally offered. "He gave the world *Women in Love* and *The Rainbow,* not to mention *Lady Chatterley's Lover.* Yes, Lawrence was a scoundrel but a genius. I think we can forgive him his infidelities." As Gabriel said this, he sucked in his belly but it still hung and nestled into the folds of the blanket. "Besides, he *understood* women. Of course he liked them."

"So," said Elisa as she kicked a stone down the slope that dead-ended at the river's edge. "If a man's a genius, he can fuck whomever he wants and belittle his wife and generally piss on people and we'll forgive him because he gave us great literature?"

Gabriel carefully put his wineglass down and sat up. He attempted to cross his legs, but abandoned the idea. Instead, he stretched them out again and leaned back on both elbows. "Dear heart, twenty years ago, I would've agreed," he said through a smile. "But, as you reach middle age, things get grayer. You forget about the little things and look at the big picture, as they say."

Elisa stood motionless, glaring at Gabriel. He shifted a bit. A rock or root prodded him in his left buttock. She was all wrong for him and he knew it. Too young. Twenty-two years too young. A goddamned sophomore. Gabriel was right to break it off. They shouldn't even be friends. He should be her professor and nothing more. Chalk it up to experience. But this nice little picnic that she had set up as a surprise. What was its purpose? No hard feelings, Professor Morales? Don't worry; I'm okay?

"Well," Gabriel finally said. "Maybe Lawrence's wife wanted it that way. Maybe she asked for it. But you're still young. You haven't had the opportunity to experience people. To really see people and what they do to themselves."

Elisa crossed her arms and shook her long black hair from her face. "You little shit!" she said, walking onto the blanket with her muddy boots. "You little condescending piece of shit!" Her left eye twitched like a finch's wing with her dark eyebrow a loosened feather about to float off.

Gabriel attempted to stand but he fell face first onto the blanket with his nose almost touching Elisa's left boot. He could smell the wet clod of earth that clung to the toe. He pushed himself up with all his strength and got on his knees. But Elisa had already turned and now she stood by the large oak searching for something.

"Elisa, dear," huffed Gabriel as he finally got to his feet. "What is all this? I thought we were going to have a nice picnic and not argue."

Elisa did not turn or acknowledge Gabriel. She suddenly stopped moving and stood still, bent a little, her head hidden by the tree.

"Elisa," said Gabriel, thinking that she was being calmed by his reasonable and reassuring voice. "Elisa, look at me. Please."

Elisa stood straight but kept her back to Gabriel. He admired her ramrod posture and the sleek, athletic contours of her neck, back, buttocks, and legs. In her big-heeled boots, she towered over him. The cool air and the rush of the Thames seemed to freeze the moment. Elisa turned and faced Gabriel. She smiled and Gabriel smiled back. Then he saw it. Elisa held a tire iron at her side. She made a low-pitched moaning sound but kept smiling. The tire iron started to shake in her hand.

Out of instinct, Gabriel turned and tried to run, but he tripped over the picnic basket, catapulting his wineglass into the air and raining Cabernet over his face and back. And then *crack-crack-crack!* Gabriel winced in pain and could no longer breathe. He lay on the crumpled basket for a moment but scrambled to his feet and turned around to look at Elisa. He clutched his left side and felt something hard and jagged protruding through his sweater.

"Start running," she said still smiling. "Start running now."

And he did. Gabriel knew that if he didn't take this chance that Elisa offered, he might not escape. So he started. And for fifteen minutes, all he heard were his own footsteps and breathing as he stumbled through the dark with nothing more than meager moonlight to help him navigate toward safety. And then he heard other footsteps. Fast and steady. Just as Gabriel seemed to find his stride despite the pain, a cloud consumed the moonlight and he could no longer discern the muddy and uneven terrain forty yards from the Thames. He stumbled twice before realizing that the footsteps behind him were not faltering or slowing. Gabriel stood and took a long, painful breath and started again, clutching two broken ribs with his right hand and holding his left out before him in an attempt to avoid slamming into a tree. "¡Pinche cabrón!" he said through his teeth, cussing at the English countryside. The cloud finally had its fill of the moon and moved on. Gabriel could see once again and plunged ahead into the brush and woods. His legs ached and he remembered his days in high school when he ran track. The coaches called him "Gazelle." Muscular legs and a flat belly. Faster than his height should have allowed. He could move around the track like a carp slicing through calm waters. But that was twenty-five years ago. Before college. Before graduate school. Before becoming tenured at Stanford. Before moving to England to introduce Wordsworth, Brontë, and Swinburne to the Stanford students who made their temporary home at the mansion known as Cliveden at Buckinghamshire. And before dining six nights a week on shepherd's pie and Guinness at the Feather's Lodge. Everyone at Feather's knew him and said he looked like a young, though darker, Richard Burton. Now his belly hung over his belt like a Hefty garbage bag filled with overcooked couscous and his lean, muscular legs had atrophied to nothing more than baseball bats wrapped in mottled skin. Gabriel clumsily ran and stumbled and crawled and scratched trying to find his way to safety.

The Thames's rushing sound grew fainter but the footsteps did not. Ah! The rose garden! Even through his cracked and muddy glasses, he could see it. The sight of the roses burning dark red in the moonlight was a beacon to the gravel path that led to the mansion's entrance and to others, to the students, to light and safety. Gabriel suddenly found his old self as his adrenal glands kicked into higher gear and he jumped over a hedge, landing solidly on his feet among the roses and swiping them aside with his left arm. The thorns ripped through his sweater, shirt, and skin, but he pushed on. The sweet, pungent smell of the roses filled his aching lungs. And he still heard the footsteps.

Gabriel's feet finally found the gravel road and he scurried toward the mansion where he could now see through the long, narrow windows. The electric lights from within Cliveden glowed warm and yellow and cast long shadows throughout the outdoor stone entryway. A dozen or so students rehearsed *Rosencrantz and Guildenstern Are Dead* with a frustrated Professor Tilden from Oxford who looked like a female Henry Higgins ranting over twelve Eliza Doolittles. Only a week before performing it for the locals. Though almost to safety, he stopped running at the edge of the entryway, at the edge of the gesticulating shadows. Gabriel turned despite himself and saw Elisa, clear under the moonlight not more than ten yards away, smiling and swinging a tire iron above her head in a circular fashion. He swiveled back to the mansion and let out a deep loud cry that made Professor Tilden and her students jerk their heads from their scripts to search out the moonlit evening.

Part Five

Professor Tilden's mahogany desk sat heavy and mournful in the middle of her office like an ancient sarcophagus. The room could have used a carpet to protect them from the cold hardwood floor. The first movement of Brahms's Piano Concerto no. 1 in D Minor meandered from a miniature RCA stereo and slowly filled the room. Gabriel leaned against the desk and surveyed its surface, his head cocked to the left, as Professor Tilden click-clacked, click-clacked in her heels away from him toward the door. Gabriel's eyes roamed the neat hills and valleys of student bluebooks, four framed photographs of one Siamese cat, two leather cups filled neatly with pencils and pens, and three paperweights sitting on nothing but the polished wooden surface of the desk. A small brass lamp saved the room from the dark night. Click-clack, click-clack and Professor Tilden, breathing hard, stood before Gabriel.

"There, my dear," she said. "The door's locked so we won't be interrupted by a stray student who can't sleep."

She leaned into him and removed his glasses, placing them on the desk. Gabriel pulled her closer. She smelled like cigarettes and strawberries. As she tried to kiss him on the lips, Gabriel slid his face past hers, rested his chin on her shoulder, and allowed his hands to start their job. He closed his eyes and lifted Professor Tilden's heavy shroudlike skirt and as he eased his right hand into the top of her panties he imagined that his long fingers were five serpents slithering toward sanctuary in the soft, moist earth. Suddenly Gabriel's eyes popped open and he stared into other eyes—by the door—eyes that were masculine, stern, and deep-set, hovering over a straight nose and a handlebar mustache. Gabriel squinted. Seeing this pale countenance startled Gabriel but the late Viscount remained safely frozen on the canvas set in an ornate gilded frame. Gabriel let out a heavy breath and focused on the portrait. Professor Tilden let out a moan. And the Viscount's eyes said to Gabriel: *This is good, Professor Morales. Finally you have a woman who is your intellectual match, your equal, your age. This is how it should be.* Gabriel shut his eyes tightly to stop the Viscount's lecture. "Elisa," he moaned.

Professor Tilden's body became rigid under Gabriel's hands. She pulled back and shook her head slowly from side to side. "What did you call me?" she said in a monotone.

Gabriel cleared his throat and rubbed his fingers together. "Sweetheart," he gently whispered. "I said 'Elizabeth.' Why do you ask?"

He moved closer to her and tried to caress her right breast. She let him. Professor Tilden kept her eyes open and reached out to Gabriel's hips and pulled him close. She opened her mouth and this time Gabriel brought his mouth to hers and kissed her. And then she stopped suddenly and let out a little shriek.

"Gabriel, there was someone in the window!"

Gabriel swiveled to look but saw only trees and bushes. "Are you sure?" he said. His hands grew wet and cold. "Are you sure?"

"Yes."

"Who was it?"

"I don't know. A woman, I think."

Gabriel walked around the desk and leaned his face close to the cold window. His breath formed a large circle of condensation, making his search that much more difficult. He squinted, but without his glasses he could discern very little. Gabriel pulled the heavy curtains closed and turned to Professor Tilden.

"It's OK," he said. "It's OK."

Part Four

"Gabe?"

"Not 'Gabe.' Please. I prefer 'Gabriel.' "

"Gabriel?"

"Yes, Elisa."

"So, that's it?"

"Yes."

"No more?"

"No more."

"Why?"

"Mutability."

"Mutability?"

"You know. The ability to change."

"I know what 'mutability' means."

" 'A musical but melancholy chime . . .' "

"Coleridge?"

"No. Wordsworth."

"Which sonnet?"

" 'Mutability.' "

"Oh. Gabe?"

"Not 'Gabe.' Please. It's 'Gabriel.' "

"Gabriel?"

"Yes, Elisa."

"Fuck you."

"Now, now, Elisa."

"No, really. Fuck you."

Part Three

"The functions of nature in Old and Middle English literature usually fall under one of two categories," Gabriel intoned to the students as they sat scribbling away in their notebooks. "First," he said, raising his right index finger into the air as if it was a revolver, "nature may act as a gift from God for man to utilize and enjoy." He hated this stuff. But he promised Professor Tilden that he would cover for her so she could leave early for London to visit her sick father. "This concept can be seen in 'The Cuckoo Song' and 'Dream of the Rood.'" He thanked God that he had saved his notes from a survey course he taught in '73 because Professor Tilden's were impossible to understand on any level. "The second function," and his middle finger joined the index, "we see in 'Battle of Maldon' and 'The Wanderer,' where nature appears to act in a malevolent manner so that the God-quality is not quite apparent."

Gabriel dropped his hand and let the students catch up with him. He scanned the room looking for opportunities. Suddenly Gabriel's visual research came to a halt when one of the dozen students shot an arm up like a mortar. She kept her head down and kept on writing with her black hair veiling her face. Before Gabriel could give permission, she stopped writing, head still down, and said, "But how can you compare these four works? Each touches on a different subject. They're too different from each other to compare, don't you agree?"

Gabriel felt blood rise into his face as he prepared to put this student in her place but stopped as she finally lifted her head from her notebook. She was exquisite. Gabriel caught his breath and coughed. He walked to her.

"And your name is?" He tried to sound nonchalant.

"Elisa, Professor Morales," she answered.

"Elisa," Gabriel said allowing the sound of her name to fill his mind. "Elisa, you make a good point, though I'm not certain that I fully agree. But why don't you explain your position a bit more?" He walked back to his desk and sat down with a loud squeak.

Elisa looked around at her expectant classmates and then back at Gabriel. "Well," she began, "take 'The Cuckoo Song' for instance. There, God's gifts are praised."

"Go on," said Gabriel intrigued by this beautiful student.

"And in 'The Dream of the Rood' Christ's agony on the cross is revealed to a dreamer. Then you mentioned 'The Battle of Maldon.' That's a historical piece. You know. A battle between the Vikings and the British."

Gabriel smiled. "And what about 'The Wanderer'?"

Elisa's brown eyes opened wide and she lifted her pencil straight into the air. "Well, there, some lonely guy relates his lament. So you see, how can you compare the interpretation of nature in any of these when they're so different in subject?"

Gabriel opened the desk drawer and rummaged around for a moment. He then pulled out a rubber band and a paper clip. He held them up, one in each hand. The entire class focused on him. "Elisa," he said gently. "Can you compare these to each other?"

Elisa blushed and looked around the classroom. The other students turned to her in unison. "What do you mean?" she finally asked.

"Can you compare this paper clip to this rubber band?"

"Well, if I tried, yes, I think I could."

"Try. For me."

Elisa coughed. "Okay. They both hold things together."

Gabriel remained motionless, his arms frozen in midair. "Go on. How are they different from each other?"

"One is soft and the other rigid. One is dull, the other shiny." Elisa's eyes watered a little.

"Ah," said Gabriel, dropping the objects on the desk. "Sometimes comparing different things can make those things clearer in our minds. Don't you think?"

Elisa cleared her throat. "Yes."

Gabriel looked at his watch. "Class over. It's been a great deal of fun. But Professor Tilden comes back Friday."

Groans emanated from all the students except Elisa. Then shuffling, bantering, and laughter filled the small room. Elisa slowly walked up to Gabriel as the other students walked past her. A young man whispered to her as they headed in different directions, "Way to go, Elisa." She winced but kept her eyes trained on Gabriel as she approached him. Gabriel sat at his desk pulling his notes together and trying not to look up.

When the room was almost empty, Elisa said, "I enjoyed your lecture."

Gabriel lifted his head slowly. She stood close enough for him to smell her perfume. "I wasn't trying to be cruel, you know."

Elisa smiled. "I know. You were right. It was a good response to my question."

"But you *did* have a point. Really. You're not completely off track." Gabriel snapped his battered leather briefcase closed and stood up not more than two feet from her. There was a momentary silence. "Elisa?"

"Yes?"

"Care to grab a drink?"

Elisa's left eye twitched. She looked around the room. It was at the farthest end of the mansion, away from the rooms that had been converted into bedrooms for the students and the Stanford faculty. The British faculty stayed in their own homes in London and commuted to Cliveden as necessary. The ancient heating system clicked repeatedly and the afternoon chill stubbornly hovered in the air. Elisa put her hand on her eye to cover up the twitch, but Gabriel had already noticed it.

"Sure," she said.

"I have some very nice sherry in my room," ventured Gabriel. His groin grew warm as he made this suggestion. He inched a bit closer to her.

Elisa turned to him. "Okay. Right now?"

"Why not?"

She did not answer but, instead, turned on her heel and walked toward the door. Gabriel followed, swinging his briefcase back and forth by his side.

Part Two

Professor Masterson rubbed his sweaty palms on the sides of his well-worn brown corduroy trousers before raising his plump, short-fingered hands up in the air and moving them as if he were playing patty-cake with an invisible friend. "Please, students, please. We must begin." His red little beak of a nose barely held his reading glasses in place and his sparse white fringe of hair flew out in various directions and looked in danger of leaving his head altogether in the very near future. "Please, we must begin."

The eighty students slowly began to find places to position themselves. The cold, cavernous room began at one end with a gargantuan mouth of a fireplace and ended at the winding stairway leading up to the students' quarters. Some sat on the floor and others perched in two-hundred-year-old chairs and couches, while still others remained standing along the walls by the tapestries and armor. Professor Masterson reached down to a student who had found a comfortable seat by the fireplace and snatched a small piece of stationery from her.

"Students," Professor Masterson finally said, "welcome to Stanford University's overseas studies program in Britain. You should each have one of these," and he held up the paper dated March 7, 1980.

There was a rustling sound and some laughter, but each student dutifully found his or her own miniature letter.

"Do not lose this!" said Professor Masterson, shaking the letter in a trembling hand for emphasis. "This certifies your participation in the program. And please note the last paragraph: 'In the event that this student leaves behind unmet financial obligations in Britain, Stanford University will cover those debts and take full responsibility for collection from the student.' "

This evoked great laughter. Professor Masterson did not smile. He handed the note back to the student and cleared his throat while shoving his hands into his pockets. "This is not a license to run up bills that you cannot meet. Do not disappoint us or your parents."

"Can I buy you a drink?" shouted one of the male students to great laughter.

Professor Masterson shook his head. "Please, I only have a few things to say and I'd like to introduce the faculty for this quarter."

The room finally grew quiet. "Most of you are majoring in English," he began. "But this is a wonderful program for any major. You will be living here in this mansion, simply known as Cliveden in Buckinghamshire. George Villiers, 2nd Duke of Buckingham, erected the first version of the mansion in the late 1600s. Part of its allure is that it stands above the Thames. Cliveden was—and is—known for its magnificent gardens. Before having his architect start any blueprints, the Duke planted woods and laid out gardens on the previously barren chalk clifftops. In the last 300 years, Cliveden survived a devastating fire and flourished through numerous redesigns and enlargements at the hands of various earls and lords. The 2nd Viscount Astor finally, in 1942, donated it to the National Trust, but Cliveden remained the home of the family until his son's death in 1966. The viscount wished for Cliveden to be used to 'bring about a better understanding between the English-speaking peoples.' So since 1969,

Stanford has leased it from the National Trust throughout the academic year to house eighty or so students each quarter."

After he finished his little speech, one that he had given countless times, Professor Masterson turned to the faculty members who stood quietly by one of the large windows near the entryway. He pointed to them and said, "We have assembled a fine group of professors from both Stanford and Oxford. They are, from my right, Professors Elizabeth Tilden, Howard Deeker, and James Spencer-Hall from Oxford and Professors Gabriel Morales, Robert Hendricks, and Gail Linnerson from Stanford." Each of the professors took a little bow when his or her name was announced. "Professor Morales has been here longest now for, how long, Gabriel?"

"Five years."

"Yes. Five years. He started teaching at Stanford fifteen years ago as a young untenured instructor. He was one of my students as an undergrad."

"Was I ever that young?" asked Gabriel to laughter.

"We were all young once, eh, Gabe?" Professor Masterson continued: "And our newest members are Professor Hendricks and Professor Tilden." They each nodded. Professor Tilden glanced at Gabriel but he kept his eyes trained on the students.

Professor Masterson wiped his brow with a handkerchief though the room remained chilly despite the presence of eighty students. He pointed to the large table at the far end of the room by the staircase. On the table sat bottles of wine and platters of cheese, crackers, and cold sliced beef. "We have a nice little treat to begin your stay here. So I'm done with my introductions. Please partake of this fine repast."

The students cheered and noisily made their way to the food.

"Yes," said Professor Masterson, "this should be a wonderful quarter."

The professors hung back for a few minutes until the hungry group of students slowly dispersed throughout the room with their wine and food.

Professor Masterson looked at the students with great pride. "A wonderful quarter," he said again to no one in particular as he shuffled toward the table for a drink.

Part One

"Mi cielo, come here," she said. Her dress pulled tightly on her ample breasts and hips. The noise made by a jumble of jangling silver bracelets on both her wrists frightened Gabriel. "Come to your tía and give her a big hug!"

Gabriel's mother nudged him. "Mijo, give your tía a big abrazo. Go on, mijo!"

Gabriel moved slowly toward his aunt. He had already perspired so much that his new white shirt, bought especially for his ninth birthday, nearly dripped in the late May heat. Numerous relatives and friends filled the backyard. Some even traveled to Los Angeles from other cities like San Diego and Bakersfield. Though World War II had ended two years ago, a few of the young men still wore their uniforms, sharp and clean and handsome. This was a special day. Not only did Gabriel turn nine, but his older sister, Estella, was graduating from St. Agnes High School and had a wonderful job lined up as a secretary at the Metro-Goldwyn-Mayer Studios. Estella's English was nothing less than perfect and she could type eighty-five words a minute. Gabriel's parents could not have asked for more. So they planned this huge pachanga and everyone who had any connection to either the Morales or Soto side of the family got an invitation.

Gabriel found his way through the partygoers and finally reached his aunt. She threw her arms open and pulled him close. She whispered into his ear, "How's my big man?" Her breath smelled like beer and her bracelets dug into Gabriel's shoulders as she hugged him tighter and tighter. "Show me your room, mi cielo. I want to see where my big man lives."

Gabriel led his aunt into the house—though she already knew her way—through the kitchen and living room, which was filled with laughter and smoke and Glenn Miller. They reached his room and went in. She closed the heavy wooden door and suddenly silence descended on them with a click of the lock. The party disappeared. Gabriel sat on his bed and his aunt walked over to his bookshelves. She let her hard red nails slide across the books' bindings, making a muffled clicking sound. Twain, Cather, Scott, and Carroll.

"Do you read all these books?" she asked, genuinely impressed.

"Yes, tía." Gabriel shifted and the bed let out a creak.

She turned and said, "No more 'tía.' It makes me feel old. Please. You can call me by my name. You know my name, don't you, mi cielo?"

"Yes, tía."

"Then use it, mi cielo."

"Okay. Graciela."

"It sounds beautiful coming from you." She pulled a pack of cigarettes from her purse and quickly lit one with a silver lighter. Her wet, narrow eyes searched the small but neat room for a makeshift ashtray. All she could find was a miniature ceramic sombrero with the words OLVERA STREET, USA painted in red block letters on the upturned brim. Without asking permission, she picked it up, flipped it over, and flicked a little ash in it. Gabriel almost let out a yelp but he kept still. His tía frightened him. She walked over to the bed and sat next to Gabriel, making the mattress sag. Gabriel tried his best not to fall against his aunt, but he failed and she caught him with her left arm and hugged him tightly, pulling his face into her ample chest.

"Oh, mi cielo, I love you so much! You're such a little man. You're going to break a lot of hearts some day." She finally released Gabriel and he scrambled to higher ground at the other end of the mattress.

She took a long drag on her cigarette and let the white smoke leak from her nostrils and mouth. She looked like a ferocious medieval monster to Gabriel. She glanced at him, smiled, and smashed her cigarette into a little ball in the ceramic sombrero. It made a sizzling sound. "Come here," she said. "Stand up and come over here," and she pointed to a spot immediately in front of her knees.

Gabriel complied. She looked him over from the top of his head to his shiny black shoes. "So handsome," she said softly. She removed some lint from his shoulder and then smoothed the front of his moist shirt, moving slowly down his chest and stomach toward his belt buckle. Gabriel closed his eyes and tried to swallow but his mouth felt as dry as burlap. "So handsome," she said again. Gabriel shut his eyes tighter and he felt his belt loosen and then heard his pants unzip. "So handsome."

Gabriel's mind fell back into an abyss. It flew down deep into darkness, far into embarrassment and powerlessness. To a place he had visited too often. So often that he couldn't remember when he had started going there. But Gabriel didn't want to go to that place again. This time, drawing on all the strength in his little body, he willed himself up into a different place. To a place safe and near a beautiful river like a picture he had seen in one of his books. Lush with thick, verdant trees, bushes, and grass on both banks and the river making a calm and constant rushing sound. And the harder he breathed, the more he became lost in the wet, clean smell of that new safe place. A place all his own. A place far from others.

JORGE, GET THE GUN

Jorge, get the gun.

¡Cabrón! Shut the fuck up!

Jorge, get the gun!

This time, Jorge turns and slaps Ricardo on the forehead: *smack!* Ricardo jumps back, stumbles on his gleaming wing tips, and slides on his left shoulder down the brick wall, ripping his dress shirt. Jorge tries to catch Ricardo but he can't. Ricardo lands on his ass in some dog piss.

¡Lo siento, mi amor! says Jorge as he reaches for Ricardo. He cradles Ricardo's head with his right hand and rubs Ricardo's groin with the other. Lo siento, whispers Jorge.

I know, mi cielo, says Ricardo. I know. But you should get the gun.

Yes.

It's over there by the tire.

Yes.

Over there, Ricardo points.

I'll get it, whispers Jorge. Jorge helps Ricardo up and straightens Ricardo's tie. I'll get it, he says again.

Jorge looks left, then right. Pico Boulevard is quiet for a change. Everyone is glued to his TV set watching JFK's funeral procession. No one knows that Mr. Saperstein is also dead behind the main cash register at Peter Pan's Grocery Store. No customers. No employees. Just the owner. Everyone is mourning the dead Catholic president. Jorge and Ricardo figure it would be easy. But Saperstein fights back. Jorge gets angry. Slaps Saperstein. Pinche Jew! Saperstein falls to the floor. Ricardo is yelling, Stop! Just get the pinche money! Jorge says,

119

shut the fuck up, maricón! This fucker dies! And Saperstein does. Bullet in his right eye, through the lens of his eyeglasses. Dead. Ricardo screams. Jorge says, Shut the fuck up! Get the money. And they do. All $59 worth. They run.

And this is where it happens. They scramble across Pico Boulevard and Jorge drops the gun. It skitters across the asphalt—*chick, chick, chick!*—and rests by a shiny Buick's tire. They keep on running and cower at the side of the building. They hide but no one is there to see them anyway.

Jorge, get the gun.

¡Cabrón! Shut the fuck up!

Jorge, get the gun!

Clip-clop, clip-clop. The horses pull the president's casket. Clip-clop, clip-clop.

Jorge, whispers Ricardo through his teeth. Get the gun.

RAMONA

irdlike. That's what she was. Don't be turned off by the cliché. I mean, look, I hate a cliché as much as the next teacher, but I can't think of a better way to describe her. Her name was Ramona. Small, frail she was. Beautiful auburn hair. Exotic plumage, really. She cocked her head like a finch, small but piercing eyes hooked into yours, blinking more than a person should. And she listened, head at a sharp angle, absorbed your words like a new sponge. Yes, Ramona was birdlike in her size, movements, and looks. But birds don't do things out of character. They do bird things. They don't go bowling. They never drive a '57 Buick. And they never—I mean never—empty a borrowed revolver into their ex-boyfriends. I am right, aren't I? If you saw a bird doing something completely out of character, you'd say to yourself, that's not very birdlike. So, one day, Ramona did something very unbirdlike. And, yes, it involved a borrowed revolver and her ex-boyfriend. Wish it involved bowling and that classic Buick. But we can't change the past, as they say. Unfortunately, we can't see the future, either.

I don't want to get into a long, detailed, and overly involved monologue about her. I've been through it too many times. With the police, and then Ramona's public defender, and that God-awful trial during one of the hottest Augusts Los Angeles has ever seen. And now I'm talking about it with this ghostwriter, a very serious and successful gentleman from New York assigned to me by my publisher. Eugene is his name. Fortyish, trim, a full head of salt-and-pepper hair, divorced and dapper with these really great bow ties that match his suspenders. I told my publisher that I could write it myself particularly because I majored in English and I'm a teacher. I've also had this dream all my life of becoming a writer, though lately what I really want is a raise, some respect from my seventh graders, a better relationship with Mama, and maybe—*maybe*—a nice guy who would be my soul mate, with or without the marriage license, and perhaps a baby or two. I don't ask for much. Not really. Eugene would even do if he weren't almost twenty years my senior. He's sweet, really, but pretty down to business with tape recorder and notepad always at the ready.

I hope you aren't getting the wrong impression. I'm not a cold person. I loved Ramona, I really did. But when you face what I did, and then face it again and again and again, you start to numb up and the tears just won't flow anymore. And then you get philosophical. And finally you get realistic: you remember the good things and put away the bad stuff because if you didn't, you'd go nuts. You teach yourself how to compartmentalize. The way President Clinton did with Monica Lewinsky. You know, sex (or "intimate non-sex") with the intern stays in this part of my brain, running the free world in this part, hugging Hillary over there. You have to do it or else you sink.

The facts concerning Ramona's case are not so unusual, in all actuality. What made it news was what she did *after* she killed Jesús. Everything else leading up to and including the shooting kind of makes sense in retrospect. Ramona and I met three years ago when she was finishing up her third year at USC Law School and I had just gotten my new job teaching the seventh grade at St. Agnes a few blocks from the university. There's this Jack-in-the-Box on Vermont by my school and I was ordering a couple of tacos when I got bumped from behind. I turned and there she was, tiny with a pixie haircut and a backpack that was way too large and out of control. She looked up at me, cocked her head just a bit, and said, "Sorry." I told her it was no problem and asked her what she carried in that backpack, rocks or something? She laughed and we ended up having lunch together.

Those first few weeks of our new friendship were wonderful and playful. She became the sister I never had and I became her only family in California. You see, Ramona ran away from home when she was sixteen. Left her parents in Tucson and headed straight for Los Angeles. She could've ended up on the streets and dead at nineteen but she had a remarkable mind and did all she could to finish high school and then Cal State L.A. Every teacher who came in contact with Ramona marveled at her intelligence and they all wanted to help her succeed. After graduating from college, she worked for about ten years at various jobs but none of them really used her brain. So she got this idea of going to law school. Came to her in a dream, she told me. Ramona contacted all of her favorite professors and they jumped in to help. It worked. Getting into USC Law School can only be described as a true-to-life example of the American dream. Imagine: this little Chicana runaway was going to become a damn lawyer! My God, she put me to shame. I didn't grow up rich or anything but at least I had Mama and, until recently, my wonderful Papa. And all I ever did was complain about how hard my life was.

But her life wasn't all American Pie, as they say. She kept secrets. I think Ramona listened to people so carefully because she didn't want to talk about herself. For example, after three months of our friendship, I finally got to see her apartment. They were fumigating my little place and I needed a place to grade papers. I didn't want to go to the library or the coffee shop so I begged her to let me use her place. She freaked out when I asked. I swear she started to shiver and her eyes got wet but she couldn't come up with an excuse.

It was a cool October afternoon when I pulled up in front of her place on 25th Street. It wasn't too bad looking, really. An old-fashioned two-story duplex with columns and a wonderful wooden porch. She rented the upper floor, which had an entrance on the side. So I went up the stairs and knocked hard on the door. I heard voices inside. I leaned closer to the door, trying to hear what was going on. An argument. I jumped almost ten feet when the door suddenly swung open and this young, beautiful, but mean-looking woman grunted past me. For one second we looked at each other and I felt shackled by her green eyes as if she knew she could crumple me up like a Kleenex. Oh my God, I thought. Ramona's a lesbian! Well, this woman whizzed by me with a laugh. I looked in and saw Ramona sitting in a ball, a small ball, in the corner of an oversized blue couch.

"Domestic problem?" I smiled, trying to be as hip and liberal as I could. Ramona wiped her eyes with a little fist.

"My daughter will be the end of me," she whispered.

Daughter! My God! The woman who had left two seconds ago was exactly that, a woman. Ramona could see what I was thinking.

"I had her when I was seventeen," she began slowly. "Nancy turned seventeen last week."

But that was it. She offered no more information other than to apologize for my seeing the tail end of the mother/daughter argument. Can you imagine? I thought we were close and I had to find out that she had a kid in this way? You can imagine that I felt a little cheated, a bit betrayed. But what can you do? Ramona was Ramona. Despite this, she surprised me again two weeks later when I just happened to meet her boyfriend, Jesús. A planner with the City of Santa Monica. Cute guy, very preppy, with skin the color of almonds and hair that glistened an impossible black. He was also ten years Ramona's junior—my age to be exact. We eventually became pretty good friends and actually had coffee once or twice alone. Jesús. God, I miss him.

Well, I said I couldn't get too deep into it all again. Not now. I'm too tired of it and I have to save what I've got for the book. Let me just say that the trial was horrible. I had to testi-

fy because I was the last one to talk to her before she killed
Jesús. Basically, what came out was that she and Jesús broke
up, I mean, he broke up with Ramona. Seems her daughter was
causing trouble, hated Jesús. And he couldn't take it anymore.
Told Ramona that she had to choose—him or her daughter.
What a choice. But she couldn't decide and so he left her.

A week after he ended it, they agreed to meet at the
Natural History Museum and talk. Ramona also had a birthday gift to give Jesús. She pulled into the parking lot across
from the museum and saw him leaning against his VW. He
walked over to her—at least that's what the parking attendant
said—real slow, smiling and waving. She got out, waved,
opened her trunk, and pulled out a beautifully wrapped present. He took it and pecked Ramona on her cheek. She turned
and looked back into the trunk. Now at this point the attendant had turned away. But the next thing he heard was a bang
and he looked up and saw Jesús lying face down on the
ground and Ramona shaking, crying, holding a gun.

But this is the weird part. The part that got her convicted
of murder instead of manslaughter. I mean, a heat of passion
thing could save you from the death penalty. The attendant
said that Ramona suddenly stopped shaking, wiped her eyes,
and then emptied the gun into Jesús's back. She then dropped
the gun, fell to her knees, and waited for the police to come.
It made all the papers. Here was this American Dream girl,
pretty and liked, dating a fine member of Santa Monica's
municipal government, and she commits cold-blooded murder
at the Natural History Museum. The stuff of tabloids.

I had to testify because, well, I'm the one who loaned her
the gun. As I told the judge and jury, she was afraid after
Jesús broke up with her because he used to stay over there a
lot. She hated sleeping alone. She had nightmares. So, Ramona
knew I had a gun and asked to borrow it. Why not? She was
so nonviolent, or so I thought. Complete pacifist. There was
no reason for me not to trust her with a gun. So, a few hours

before she was to meet Jesús for lunch, Ramona swung by my place and I gave her the gun. No one blamed me.

I couldn't tell them everything that we talked about that day. It could be misconstrued. You know lawyers. She was afraid of being alone, that's true. But she also told me that she was so angry with Jesús that she felt crazy sometimes. She thought something was going on behind her back but she didn't know what. I didn't tell anyone she said this. I also never testified that I told Ramona that you can't trust men. If you give them an inch, well, you know. I told her that sometimes men need to be taught a lesson. They're basically animals, you know, looking for the next bitch to fuck. That's what I told Ramona the day she killed Jesús. And when I said that, she smiled and said she understood.

Birds don't do certain things, you know. They do bird things. They don't kill their ex-boyfriends. And they don't take the stand in their own defense.

REAL TIME

D iana saw it. So did her two roommates, Avram and Raquel. And it saw them. For but a second, maybe two, their six human eyes widened and locked onto its wild but somehow controlled eyes. The gray sky muted the colors of the trees, grass, birds—everything—so that they weren't quite certain they were seeing what they were seeing. The three humans squinted in unison. Even *it* seemed to squint back at them.

"Oh, my God," said Diana. She held the platter of steaming Spanish rice in front of her like a mispositioned shield. Her nose itched but she dared not put the platter down.

"Let's get closer to it," said Raquel.

Without moving his head, Avram's eyes shifted over to Raquel. "No," he whispered.

Realizing what they were looking at, Diana said almost as an apology, "I thought it was a possum or a raccoon or something."

With this last utterance, its ears perked, and its taut golden body froze in mid-stride. The family of quail that only a moment ago scurried nearby was nowhere to be found. Raquel shifted her left foot toward the low metal fence that separated nature from their trimmed, controlled backyard, but Avram grabbed her shoulder before she moved her other foot. He could feel Raquel's toned muscles through her thick Gap oxford shirt. Before Avram could offer a verbal warning, it turned its head from them and, with nonchalance so palatable that it seemed to mock the humans, the creature disappeared into the hilly shrub. Within moments it was out of sight. A fat, noisy crow dove down from their roof and perched on the fence feeling brave now that the predator had moved on.

"A mountain lion," whispered Avram, still holding Raquel's shoulder.

"Let go," growled Raquel, but he didn't.

"In Los Angeles?" Diana murmured. "How can that be?"

"West Valley," corrected Raquel. They all kept their eyes locked onto the spot where the animal had stood. "People haven't completely destroyed the natural habitat up in these hills."

"Well, you're enjoying this beautiful house, so how can you complain?" laughed Avram.

"I'm only renting, like you," said Raquel as she shrugged Avram's hand off her shoulder. They all finally looked at each other.

Avram laughed again and reached for the large blue plastic bowl of Doritos that sat on the overburdened card table. Popping a crispy triangle of fried fake tortilla into his mouth with a crunch, he said, "Oh, *that* makes a difference. I must have missed that class taught by your favorite Commie professor. Velasco? Right? Professor Jaime Velasco?"

"No se hizo la miel para la boca del asno," whispered Raquel. She turned quickly and went into the house. The crow let out an impossibly loud squawk and flew off into the gray sky.

"Nice job," said Diana.

"What did she say to me?"

Diana sighed. "She said that you were the biggest jerk to get into UCLA Law School." She put the platter down for emphasis. The plastic forks and knives rattled and the lemonade in the perspiring pitcher rocked back and forth in little waves.

"No, she didn't."

Diana's nostrils flared. "The chicken is burning. Go apologize to Raquel."

"No." Avram crossed his arms over his broad chest. He stood almost a full foot taller than both his roommates.

"Go and I'll pull the chicken from the barbecue before it's totally ruined."

They stood in silence for six seconds. Avram uncrossed his arms. Now he could smell something burning. "Okay, okay. I'll say sorry to my little Communist roommate."

"Good. And cut out that 'Commie' crap. It's even beginning to bug me."

Avram went into the house. Beads of perspiration formed on his upper lip and he grew angry at himself because he could feel his groin grow warm. The slight chance of being alone with Raquel still sent a thrill through his body even though they'd known each other since their first year of law school and he knew deep down nothing would ever happen between them. Avram walked across the beautiful hardwood floor, past the kitchen, dining room, and living room and toward the staircase. Renting this gorgeous four-bedroom home was the smartest thing he had ever thought of. It was their last year of law school, he argued during one of their study sessions last year, and they should make the most of it, live in a real house together, not separately in identical seven-hundred-square-foot Westwood studio apartments for $1,000 per month, roaches included. Sure, the commute on the 101 and then, God, the 405, would be a pain, but imagine studying constitutional law or preparing for interviews up in the hills with a view of the Valley and a pool thrown in for good measure. Only $3,000, including utilities, split three ways. Imagine!

"A pool?" Raquel had asked in disbelief. "An actual swimming pool?"

Avram offered a smile, hoping that he looked handsome to her. "Yep, a swimming pool." He imagined what it would be like to sit back and watch Raquel in a tiny one-piece swimsuit just lounging about in the sun.

"How could it be so cheap?" asked Diana, rubbing her nose with a closed yellow highlighter.

"The guy doesn't want to sell yet," said Avram, trying not to sound too enthusiastic. "But he wants to move to a smaller place. His wife died a couple of years ago and his kids are out on their own. He's rattling around that place and just wants to make enough on a lease to maintain his puny mortgage payments."

Raquel turned to Diana. "A pool, Di. A pool." So, that sunny afternoon in May of last year, Avram convinced Raquel and Diana that his idea was nothing short of brilliant.

He reached the staircase and started up but then froze. He heard something. And it scared him. The hair on his neck and arms rose in some kind of primal alarm. Avram cocked his head to the left and then to the right, holding his breath to be as quiet as possible, and listened. At first it didn't sound human. It reminded him of something he had heard in a nature documentary: a high-pitched whine, like an animal in pain. What was it?

"Raquel?" he called out. The noise stopped suddenly. He then heard footsteps, Raquel's bedroom door open, more footsteps, and then the smaller bathroom door shut. The noise started again. In slow motion, Avram walked backwards, down the steps, and got to the landing. The sound had come from Raquel. "My God," he whispered. "My God."

Camera Two:

"No se hizo la miel para la boca del asno," whispered Raquel. She turned quickly and went into the house. Early Eric Clapton blasted on the stereo (Avram's choice), which propelled her faster through the house toward the staircase. *Why did he grab me like that?* she thought. That innocent gesture opened something in her and she couldn't stop it. Raquel tried unsuccessfully to catch her breath as she groped the fine-grained banister with both hands. *Why did he grab me like that?* She hadn't slept much the last four or five days. She was at wit's end interviewing for jobs on campus. Raquel pulled herself up the stairs. Her mind entered a cloud and she could see her cousin Miguel, age thirteen, staring at her naked nine-year-old body. Raquel shook her head, trying to shake the memory as she had before, but it took over all of her senses. Miguel grabbed her shoulder with his left hand, hard and mean, and he used his other hand on her. Where were her parents? How could they let him watch her? Raquel suddenly fell into the present and found herself in her bedroom, curled up, sobbing, shaking, trying to breathe.

"Raquel?" Avram called out. Raquel's trance broke and she stopped crying in an instant almost as if she had pushed the "mute" button on the remote control. She stood up, opened her bedroom door, and went into her bathroom, shutting the door behind her. She curled again into a ball, at one end of the dry bathtub, and started her sobbing again, full force.

Camera Three:

Diana watched Avram's muscular neck and back as he walked into the house. She shook her head and smiled. *I'm just a little horny right now,* she justified to herself. *Me and Avram? No way! He's too close a friend.* Diana carried a clean platter to the barbecue, opened its gleaming stainless steel lid, and started salvaging the smoking chicken by maneuvering the clacking tongs to grasp the sizzling pieces of bird. As she filled the platter, she remembered how her father, as most dads did, ruled the barbecue. Outdoor cooking was *his* domain. He fumbled at most things in life, like making a steady living or keeping his wife from leaving one early morning when Diana was fourteen, the day the space shuttle exploded over America. But when he still had a marriage (at least in his mind), he used to stand with one hand on his narrow hip, the other holding tongs like an artist's brush, sunglasses hiding brilliant blue eyes, and explain to his only child the intricacies of barbecuing. He had joked that the secrets of the art really should only be passed on from father to son, but she'd do. This made Diana laugh, understanding the joke, and she felt special.

Diana closed the barbecue, lifted the now-heavy platter, and turned to go back to the card table. But she stopped. She saw something in her peripheral vision. The mountain lion! It stood by the pool's edge, on the other side, not moving, just staring at Diana. The water rippled with the constant breeze that blew through the backyard. She knew she should be frightened, but she wasn't. Should *it* be frightened of humans? But there they stood, not more than ten yards from each other, neither one moving. She remembered that her father had said that mountain lions and pumas were, in all actuality, the same animal, just different names. But one sounded more dangerous, didn't it? *Which one?* Puma, of course. Puma is a more dangerous name, don't you think, my sweets? And which one was this? A mountain lion? A puma? She had automatically called it a mountain lion when they first saw it. But right now she wanted it to be a puma. It made her feel something. Was it a good feeling? She didn't know. She couldn't name *that*.

TABULA RASA

I shaved my mother's head yesterday."

Yesterday. That was Sunday. Elena let her words just hang there between us as I watched her clear the desk of extraneous matter—black Sharpie markers, Scotch tape, rulers—so she could make room for the new posters that we had just picked up from Kinko's. I observed her small brown hands maneuver quickly, without a wasted movement, intent on a purpose. I wanted to grab her hands, stop them, squeeze them, and make her look at me while she told me what she did yesterday. But I didn't because she'd pull away, tell me not to be so macho, a typical male. A typical *Mexican* male. And then I'd say, no, I'm Chicano and almost done with college. I'm no Neanderthal. So, instead of getting into a stupid fight, I stood silently and let her finish cleaning the desk.

When she put the last desk-thing away (a plastic paper clip holder), she leaned back and rested tight fists on her narrow hips. Elena wore her favorite baggy khakis with a skin-tight black T-shirt; the words CHICANO MUSIC AWARDS hovered over her left breast. An unruly black curl bobbed happily across her forehead and again I had to keep my hands to myself, not reach over, fix it. I think Elena knew it bothered me and let another curl find its way down. She stared down at her handiwork. Now every nick, scratch, and ink stain sat exposed on what was once an expensive piece of mahogany furniture that had probably graced some high-priced lawyer's office back in the '60s.

"There," she finally said. "Bring the posters over so we can take a good look at them."

I obeyed. I walked over to her neatly made bed and grabbed the posters. I laid the pile of light green cardboard on the desk. Elena tilted her head to the left and then to the right.

"Beautiful," she said.

I nodded. We stood in silence for about a minute.

"Mom had been warned that the chemotherapy would probably do this. You know, her hair," Elena continued as she flipped through the posters to see if there were any misprints.

"Yeah," I said. "I know." I couldn't read her expression and this bothered me. We'd been together since freshman year and I figured I could decipher every look that crossed her beautiful face.

"I was cooking breakfast and I heard her scream. I ran upstairs to her room, and I found her in bed, sitting up, with a clump of white hair clutched in her hand."

"Damn," was all I could offer.

Elena pulled a reject out of the pile and handed it to me. "I just ran and put my arms around her." She continued to thumb through the pile. "I calmed her down finally, and decided to make it nice. As nice as I could."

I put the rejected poster back on her bed. I figured we could go back to Kinko's and get a refund for each one that didn't come out right. "What did you do?" I asked.

She let out a sigh and looked at me. "I ran a hot tub, helped her in, and then very slowly clipped her hair with scissors." Elena's eyes flickered down toward the posters and she quickly pulled out another reject.

"And?"

"Then I lathered her head real gently and shaved it slowly while humming a little song she used to sing to me when I was little."

I didn't know what to think. First, the image of Elena shaving Mrs. Montes's head was almost too much for me. Second, I couldn't figure out why Elena was even here today. The posters didn't have to go up until closer to the demonstration

against the Townsend project. A huge luxury housing develop-
ment had gotten city approval despite serious environmental
concerns. Basically, the Townsend Corporation was going to
clear-cut over a thousand acres of trees, shrubs, and tall grass
to supply homes to the wealthy. We were willing to get arrested before our foothills were destroyed. We had almost eighty
students and faculty ready to converge on the site this Friday.
So we could have waited until tomorrow to put up the posters.

"The rest of these look fine," Elena announced. She
straightened them out. "Where's the staple gun?"

"I saw it in Thien's room," I said as I started toward the
door. Elena shared this small but very functional three-bedroom
house with two other female students.

"What were you doing in Thien's room?"

I stopped in my tracks but didn't turn around. "She needed some help in calculus."

Elena let out a little cough. "She has her eyes on you."

I didn't hear a hint of a laugh in her voice. "Mi amor, I'm
a one-woman man," I said and started walking again.

"And don't you forget it," she answered almost in a whisper. "My love for you is pure."

I stopped again and laughed at this overly formal pro-
nouncement, but Elena stood there without a even a shadow of
a smile on her face. We stood there frozen for a few moments.

"So is mine," I finally answered.

"Are you sure?" she said, still not showing any sign of levity.

"Of course," I snorted. "I might not be perfect, but I'm
sure of *that.*"

"Es mejor mancha en la frente que manchita en el corazón,"
Elena said, this time with the left corner of her mouth rising up
in a half-smile. One of her favorite dichos: It's better to have a
stain on one's forehead than a stain on one's heart.

I now felt that I could go and get the staple gun without
looking like a jerk. Just as I left, she raised her voice: "Thien's
room is a pigsty! How can you find anything in there?"

Elena was right but I knew where to look and went right to it. Walking back, all I could think of was Elena humming softly as she used a razor to make clean rows of smooth skin down the back of her mother's head, and in her heart, wishing that with each gentle stroke a bit of the cancer was being stripped away.

*   *   *

The sun shone brightly through the oaks. More people showed up for the demonstration than we had expected. The TV camera crews set up across from the bulldozers and we stood on the other side behind the chain link fence. My roommate, Darius, had already cut a large flap in the fence but he held it down until I gave the signal. Elena breathed heavily by my side. She carried a sign that said TREES, NOT HOUSES! Someone blasted an old Bob Dylan song on a boom box. Several men and women in dark suits milled about. I didn't know who they were, but they scared me just a bit. The Townsend work crew hadn't shown up yet, so the bulldozers sat motionless. It was noisy, like a carnival, but without the rides and cotton candy. I finally gave the signal by yelling, of all things, Charge! and Darius lifted the flap of chain link to let us in. And in we came, chanting, screaming, singing, clapping. The camera operators went into action. Within seconds, we had swarmed the bulldozers like insects in search of sustenance.

The cops finally arrived—six patrol cars in all—and surrounded the area. I lost sight of Elena but figured she'd be safe. Our plan was to cover each of the five bulldozers with bodies, and there were more than enough of us to do this. One of the officers got on a bullhorn and told us to leave the premises because we were trespassing. We just cheered, almost in unison, and packed in closer to the bulldozers.

Then it happened. Someone—I don't know who—threw something. It flew over the fence and hit the hood of a patrol car with a metal thump so loud that we all suddenly became quiet. We heard one loud *Disperse!* come from the bullhorn. Then one of the officers tossed a small metal canister over the fence. Smoke! That little can let out so much of the stuff, I couldn't believe it. And then another can came sailing over and then another. Finally, we were engulfed in stinging thick white haze. I tried to find Elena. Our group became frantic, people started to push, fall, and run toward the flap. I heard screams. Where was she?

"Clear the area!" the officer yelled through the bullhorn.

Though my eyes stung, I finally spotted Elena. She had climbed to the very top of one of the bulldozers. She had wrapped her nose and mouth in a red bandanna. I could hear her screaming, see her fist pulsating in rhythmic jabs into the smoky air. I froze. I didn't recognize the look in her eyes: wild, angry, like an animal. At that moment, I was no longer a part of her. Elena became a different person, speaking a different language, seeing a different world. I heard her voice pierce the chaos. She chanted, "A life for a tree, a life for a tree!" A strong wind blew the smoke higher so that, for a moment, I couldn't see her at all. But I could hear a voice, "A life for a tree, a life for a tree!" But I didn't know the voice anymore. I just stood there, not knowing what to do next. Not understanding what was happening.

DEVIL TALK

Ysrael Zendejas preferred to take the stairs despite the stiffness in his knees. He was still trim, straight-backed, and brown as a nut, but his high school football days finally caught up with him ten years ago. He lifted one leg after the other up toward his neat and simplified life in the brand new condominium, freshly painted and hermetically sealed, on Burbank Boulevard. Not as spacious as his split-level home in West Hills, but he didn't need all that room anymore. Ruth had died three years ago this August. On the first anniversary of her death, their son, Nathaniel, a lawyer with the Oregon Attorney General's Office, had flown down to Los Angeles for the unveiling of Ruth's tombstone and spent two full weeks helping his father find just the right place.

"You're going to go crazy wandering around this huge place all by yourself," Nathaniel had said as he spooned tortilla soup past his thin lips as the two sat in a booth at the California Pizza Kitchen. "Absolutely loco, Papa."

So it was planned a bit too fast for Ysrael's liking. Though he himself had been a lawyer for many years, he had grown somewhat passive in retirement. And then with his wife's passing, he seemed lost at times. So Nathaniel took care of everything. He even made a tidy profit for his father on the house on Valley Circle and got a good deal on the condominium two miles away. "Close to two malls, Papa," Nathaniel had said. "Topanga Plaza and the Promenade." Ysrael had offered his son a wan smile. "Me, Papa, I prefer the Promenade. They've got Macy's and a multiplex there."

Ysrael reached his floor, paused for but a moment, and breathed deeply. The hall smelled of different foods (Chinese takeout, enchiladas, pizza, some kind of fish), dinners now past. He then turned to the left and walked four doors to his unit. He pulled his key from his pocket with his left hand and touched the mezuzah with his right. Both the key and the mezuzah felt cool, solid. Ysrael brought his hand down from the mezuzah, kissed his fingertips, slid the key into the lock with a *shoonk*, and then turned it with a *cleenk*.

He settled down comfortably in his favorite recliner with a mug of decaffeinated mocha java (Ysrael was pleased to learn from his son that he could now buy Starbucks whole bean or ground at Ralph's), Vivaldi on the stereo, and the *Los Angeles Times* spread upon his lap. After no more than an hour, Ysrael dozed noisily. And he dreamed. Vibrant colors and sounds of spring swirled about him. Ruth stood there by his side, incandescent and beautiful, whispering, "I'm waiting for you, my love." A brook gurgled happily and birds flew about, in and around lush oaks, singing Vivaldi's spring (the *largo e pianissimo sempre* to be precise) with such rapture that Ysrael's heart swelled with each successive note. What must have been a woodpecker rapped softly, rhythmically, on a branch somewhere nearby. But the rapping grew louder, more deliberate, impatient. Eventually, the brook, trees, and Ruth dripped away and Ysrael's great brown eyes popped open. He was back in his den and the woodpecker's rapping moved from a disappearing tree to the front door.

"Damn!" Ysrael muttered as he pulled himself out of his chair. He walked deliberately to the door as the knocking grew louder. "I'm coming, I'm coming!" But he stopped suddenly, two feet from the door. Who could be knocking? he thought. I haven't buzzed anyone in. Must be a neighbor. Perhaps that widow Mrs. Gurley from down the hall. Probably having trouble with her dishwasher again but, in reality, she's interested in me. ¡Que lástima! That's all I need!

Ysrael took one more step and lifted his left hand to the doorknob. The smooth brass felt warm to the touch. That's odd, he thought. He turned it with a quick, irritated flick of his wrist and opened his mouth to say something rather unpleasant to Mrs. Gurley but he froze, mouth agape, once the door swung open. Before him stood a man, head tilted to Ysrael's right, away from the mezuzah, smiling and humming to the Vivaldi that was still playing on the stereo. He held a beautiful brown leather briefcase by his side.

Ysrael composed himself. "How did you get in the complex? Who buzzed you in?"

The man, who wore a finely tailored blue pinstripe suit, a gleaming white shirt, and crimson necktie, walked past Ysrael through the small foyer and into the living room where he gently lowered himself into the middle of the long green leather sofa. He placed the briefcase on his lap, snapped it open, gestured toward Ysrael's still-warm recliner and said in a soft voice, "Please sit."

Because the man easily weighed fifty pounds more than he did (the man clearly made it to the gym on a regular basis), Ysrael closed the door and went back to his recliner. As the man shuffled through his briefcase, Ysrael realized that he must be some kind of insurance salesman.

"I'm insured to the hilt," Ysrael smiled.

The man looked up and laughed a sharp little laugh. "Oh, no. I'm not selling anything. I am, however, here to bargain a bit." As he whispered this last statement, he pulled out a manila folder, closed his briefcase, and put the latter down by his radiant Bostonians. He opened the folder. "Mr. Zendejas?"

Ysrael fell back in his recliner with a shock. "Yes?"

"Mr. Jesús Zendejas?"

"No, no. Not anymore, I mean," Ysrael said through a cough. "I changed my name to Ysrael, after I converted." He didn't know why he answered this stranger at all but, for some reason, he couldn't control himself.

"Converted?"

Ysrael coughed again. "Why, yes. To Judaism. Thirty-five years ago."

The man riffled through the file. "No. That can't be. It's not in here."

"I was raised Catholic, you see. But after I met my wife, Ruth, who was a Jew, I fell in love with Judaism. I studied for years. Converted after we married."

"No," the man repeated as he put the folder down on his lap. "There's nothing of this in your file."

"It's true. I do not lie." Ysrael smiled. "I changed my name after I converted because, as you can imagine, you get a lot of strange looks at temple when you say your name is Jesús. Even if it is pronounced the Spanish way and even though Jesus Christ was a Jew himself."

The man's eyes bulged. And then, ever so slowly, his eyelids lowered and he let out a little snicker. "Ah! That explains the mezuzah. I figured it was left by the prior owner."

"No. My wife bought that for me when I converted."

"Wait until they hear about this at the home office!"

"And where's the home office?" Ysrael asked, finally getting curious again.

"Hell, of course."

At that moment, Ysrael knew he should have been startled or, at the very least, confused. Perhaps, he thought, after several decades as a criminal defense attorney, he was not shocked because he had heard millions of very strange utterances. Ysrael laughed. "Hell? That's rich."

The man returned the laugh. "Well, you see, Jes—I mean, Ysrael, you are going to die tonight in your sleep, very peacefully, and I wanted to make a little deal with you. But because you're no longer a Christian, my hands are tied." He reached for his briefcase, snapped it open, and slid the file back in.

Fear did not creep into Ysrael's heart. He was merely puzzled. "Why can't you make a deal with a non-Christian?"

"Well, you realize that Torah makes no direct reference to either heaven or hell, don't you?" He snapped his briefcase shut for emphasis, not without a little irritation.

This whole issue of the afterlife was the biggest chasm Ysrael had to leap when he started his Judaic studies all those years ago. Heaven and hell, particularly for Mexican Catholics, were as real as the nuns and priests who taught him how to be a "good" Christian. But then, reaching back to his wonderful long meetings with Rabbi Burke (as well his son's own Torah worksheets from grammar school), Ysrael said, "Ah! What of Gan Ayden and Gehenna?"

The man paused, scratched his goatee, and thought for a moment. "Hhhmmm. Interesting point, Ysrael. Interesting point. But those were concepts of Talmudic times. And, besides that, those were actual physical places here on earth. Very different from reality. *My* reality."

The man was, of course, correct. As a post-Talmudic Jew, Ysrael believed in the immortality of the soul. But as Maimonides wisely noted, there are neither bodies nor bodily forms in the world to come, only the souls of the righteous. He looked at the man and said simply, "You're right."

"I must be going," said the man as he stood up, knees cracking just a bit. "Many more trips tonight. I apologize for the inconvenience."

Ysrael stood, as well, and his knees echoed the man's. "No problem, really." Ysrael suddenly laughed. "My father used to say, 'De puerta cerrada el diablo se vuelve.' "

"Languages were never my forte," said the man.

"From a closed door, the devil goes away."

The man chuckled. "Again, Mr. Zendejas, I'm sorry about all this."

"Except that business about me dying tonight, and all, it was sort of nice having a little company. But I have two questions for you, if you don't mind."

"It's the least I can do. Shoot."

"First, by your existence, does that mean Jesus Christ was, indeed, the Messiah?"

"No. Next question."

"Yes, well . . ." Ysrael looked around and coughed a bit. "Well, what was the bargain you planned to offer?"

"Oh, that. You know. The usual. I'd bring back your wife and the two of you could live for ten happy years together."

"In exchange for my soul, I suppose."

"What else would I want?"

Ysrael rubbed his hands together. "Now that would be tempting, indeed!"

"But I can't offer it. I couldn't offer it to a Buddhist, a Muslim, an atheist, or any other non-Christian. I'm sorry. Rules are rules."

With that, the man headed toward the door, nodded a goodnight, and was gone. Ysrael sighed and sat down in his recliner. Vivaldi still played in the background. He let out another sigh, closed his eyes, and quickly fell asleep. His mind eased into the same wonderful dream he was having before the man came to visit. The lush greenery, playful brook, singing birds, and his beautiful Ruth. And in his sleep, Ysrael's heart stopped. As he slipped from this world into the next, he found himself lying in Ruth's arms as they lay in the clover.

"My love," Ruth said. "I've been waiting. What took you so long?"

Ysrael kissed Ruth's soft young cheek (for they were both in their twenties now), and noticed with delight that she smelled of fresh lemons. He said, "Oh, mi amor, I had a visitor. Please forgive me."

She pulled him closer and nuzzled his thick black hair with a laugh. "Of course, my love," she cooed. "Not another thought of it."

Muy Loca Girl

arta spied a parking space in the large lot behind the restaurant after only a few minutes of searching. The lot usually teemed with prowling SUVs and Volvos and Hondas because it also served Ralph's, Blockbuster, and many little shops. But today most people headed to either the Topanga Plaza or the Promenade for the malls' holiday price wars. Her Ford Falcon creaked as it settled into its spot and Marta pulled the emergency brake with a loud crank. She sat for a moment mesmerized by a lone gray cloud that hung over a billboard advertising a Bruce Willis movie. Willis squinted and offered Ventura Boulevard a tough but playful smile. Marta shook her head. She got out of her car, locked it, and headed to the back entrance of the deli. Marta pulled hard on the heavy glass and metal door, which eventually gave with a loud moan. She walked toward the front of the restaurant and found the hostess, a rather stout woman behind a wooden stand that held a well-worn spiral tablet. The hostess's hair resembled a haystack and a thin film of perspiration covered her upper lip and nose. Marta gave the hostess her name. The woman wielded her pencil as if it was a magic wand and smiled at Marta as she asked, "Did you say your name was 'Martha'?" After Marta corrected the hostess, she found a seat in the waiting area. "It'll only be a few minutes," the hostess said. "You're lucky, dear. You missed the crowd. Just an hour ago this place was crawling with people."

Marta sat next to a young mother who held a squirming two-year-old boy on her lap while keeping watch over her infant daughter who sat strapped in an oversized Evenflo stroller like

John Glenn in his space capsule. With her free hand the mother rocked the stroller back and forth as her baby slipped in and out of sleep. The baby breathed noisily through pouty lips; ruddy cheeks broke the smooth sameness of her creamy skin. "Laura," the hostess suddenly called out as if the young mother were many blocks away. "Your table is ready." Laura gathered up her son with one arm and pushed the stroller with the other and followed the hostess. The baby's eyes flashed open with the sudden jerk of the stroller, revealing almost translucent blue-green irises.

When the hostess came back, she said, "Martha, your table is ready, too." Marta didn't bother to correct her this time but just got up and followed. It's a simple name, she thought. Marta. Without an "h." As the hostess led her to a table, Marta made eye contact with her friend Isabel, who was taking an order from a lanky teenage boy wearing a T-shirt with the word "Outkast" emblazoned on its front. Isabel nodded and gave Marta a worried look.

Marta sat down. The hostess handed her a large menu and said, "Have a nice one," and waddled away to a waiting customer. A small man wearing an apron brought a setup and a glass of icy water. Marta said, "Gracias," and the man gave a quick smile and walked away, drying his hands on his apron. She put her hands around the sweating glass and then patted her cheeks with the cool condensation. After a few moments, Marta wiped her hands on her jeans and then pulled from her backpack some medical literature and various notes that she had scribbled on the last few pages of her calculus notebook. Suddenly, she heard Isabel and looked up. "Mija, what's wrong?" She liked to call Marta "mija" even though at twenty-two, Isabel was only two years older than her friend. "You look like shit."

"Thanks," said Marta. But she smiled because she knew only Isabel could listen to her at that moment. "Can you take a break?"

"Mija, I already told Tim that I was taking fifteen to talk to my girlfriend. He asked who it was and I said you so he said okay. That cabrón wants to get into your panties soooo baaaad!" And with that, Isabel sat down with a little grunt. She was tall with dark brown skin and long hair pulled up in a maniacal pile like some kind of Chicana Medusa trying to keep her serpents in line. Her heavy eyelids barely revealed deep brown eyes. A little black teardrop tattoo adorned the outside of her left eye. Isabel's flat nose hovered above thick lips and reminded Marta of the Aztec carvings she studied in her ancient cultures textbook last year but never saw in person. Isabel wore a tight too-short T-shirt that accentuated her breasts. A silver ring dangled enticingly from her everted belly-button. Isabel always bent the restaurant's dress code. Last week she confided to Marta that she planned to get her nipples pierced once she got enough "huevos"—as Isabel put it —to stand the pain she had read about in a piercing magazine. She already had five silver studs running along the edge of her left ear and three on the other.

A tall, skeletal waiter shuffled up to their table and took Marta's order while studiously refusing to acknowledge Isabel's presence. His hair burned an unnatural red even though it was not dyed, and freckles covered his face and bare arms as if a cruel prankster had splattered him with paint. He walked away silently after taking Marta's order of matzo ball soup and iced tea.

"Pendejo," said Isabel. "Just because I let him feel up my tits after a party he thought we were fuckin' married or something. Shit, I was drunk. ¡Chingao!" Isabel shook her head as she pondered the stupidity of men. "He stopped talking to me when he finally got the message. Not my type. Too gabacho. And you know what?" Before Marta could respond, Isabel answered, "He tried to sweet talk me by giving me this little boy look and saying, 'Yo quiero Taco Bell'! I slapped his pinche gabacho face. I think I chipped a tooth, too!"

Isabel took a drink from Marta's ice water as she picked up one of the medical pamphlets. "Mija, what the fuck is this shit?"

Marta pulled the pamphlet from Isabel and put it with the others and set them aside. "I'm sick," she said.

"What do you mean you're sick?" Isabel looked down at the medical literature and saw the word "ovarian."

"You ain't got cancer, mija?"

The waiter brought the soup and drink over. Isabel ignored him and waited for him to leave.

"No, but I am sick." Marta picked up her spoon and carved out a piece of the matzo ball and placed it gingerly into her mouth. It felt so peaceful and warm on her tongue. Isabel perched her head on her fists and looked very worried. All ten fingers glistened with silver rings. How did we ever become friends when we have nothing in common? thought Marta. In her early teens she was an inch away from being a chola in a gang. The teardrop tattoo was the last straw. It symbolized a year in jail even though Isabel had never gotten arrested, but she clearly wanted to show her allegiance to the local gangbangers. Marta had little doubt that Isabel was saved when her mother got a new job eight years ago to get them out of the Pico-Union area. They moved twenty-nine miles west to the San Fernando Valley. Isabel finished at Canoga Park High and immediately went from part-time to forty hours a week as a waitress at Solley's at Ventura and Topanga Canyon. She didn't like it much when Jerry's Famous Deli bought it out, but she stayed more out of inertia than anything else. Marta sometimes felt hopelessly naïve in Isabel's presence. She had attended Catholic schools for twelve years before enrolling at Cal State Northridge. Her parents had a solid if boring marriage. Marta's two younger brothers were doing just fine as well. Isabel introduced herself to Marta one day two years ago at Starbucks in Topanga Plaza. They'd been friends ever since.

"Mija, you better fuckin' tell me what's going on or I'm gonna kill you!" The hostess passed their table leading a thirty-something Chicano wearing an expensive blue pinstripe suit and carrying a briefcase. Isabel's head swiveled to keep him in sight. "¡Qué mono! ¿Verdad?"

Marta sighed. "Yes, he's cute but you already have Roberto."

"A girl can always trade up, mija." Isabel suddenly felt embarrassed at her inability to focus on her friend's problem just because a good-looking male had happened to wander into her sphere of consciousness. "Marta, as my Mom says, 'Cuéntale tus penas a quien te las pueda remediar,'" she offered.

Marta looked around at the other tables. Too many people, too much noise, she thought. I need to sleep, not talk. She took a deep breath. "Look, I'm trying to figure this all out. The doctor didn't even have very much information that she could give me. This problem is so new."

"What problem, mija?" Isabel leaned forward so that her nose almost touched Marta's. Suddenly Isabel threw her arms to her sides and leaned back into her chair. "This has to do with that fuckin' yuppie couple you helped out with your eggs, right?"

"Yes," said Marta.

"So, what the fuck did they do to your insides?" Isabel asked, rocking her head back and forth and jutting out her chin for emphasis.

Marta pushed her soup away to the side of the table. Her chest and abdomen ached. Marta focused her eyes on the cloudy broth that slid up and down the bowl's sides in mini-waves. "Well, they warned me that there could be side effects."

Tim the manager walked up and said hello. Isabel gave him an annoyed look and said in an exaggerated whisper, "If you give me ten more minutes, I'll give you the best blow job you've ever had. What do ya say, hombre?"

Tim blushed redder than the vinyl that covered the booths and walked away without a word.

Marta shook her head. "Isabel, how could you be so crass?"

"The pendejo loves it. Anyway, so what DO you have?"

Marta grabbed her notes. "They call it 'ovarian hyper-stimulation syndrome.'"

Isabel blinked. "What the fuck is that?"

Marta shifted in her chair. "You know how they had to harvest eggs from me?"

"Yeah. I remember calling you 'Old MacDonald' because it made me think of a farm." Marta managed a small smile. Isabel continued: "You told me that this pinche egg thing's illegal in other countries."

"Yeah," said Marta. "Canada and Israel, I think. You don't forget a thing I tell you, do you?"

Isabel gave a self-satisfied smile.

"Well, anyway, the fertility drugs that they gave me to drop a lot of eggs worked too well and I'm having a bad reaction." As Marta said this, she seemed to shrink.

"Like what, mija?" Isabel's stomach tightened.

"I'm going through . . ." and she looked at her notes again. "It's called premature menopause."

"What the fuck!" Isabel almost yelled.

"Quiet," said Marta in a whisper. "You're embarrassing me."

"You mean you helped that Chicana with her gabacho husband have twin girls with *your* eggs and now they turned you into an old woman? You should be the one screaming! That's fucked!"

"Isabel, it doesn't matter what color her husband is. Color doesn't matter."

Isabel shifted in her seat. "Look, forget that." She began again: "You got rights, mija. You gotta sue or something. If you don't, you're a muy loca girl!"

"I can't sue. I got paid $2,500 and I signed all kinds of waivers."

"There must be a way out of that shit," said Isabel. "Besides, you didn't do it for the money. You felt bad for them. I remember. That ad you saw made you cry and you told me that you could have your niños later."

Marta just sat there. Her physical demeanor and shape contrasted dramatically with that of Isabel. Marta was barely five feet tall with a tight, well-controlled haircut. Unlike Isabel, she wore little make up and her features were fine, almost Asian, and she wore simple gold studs, one in each ear. Marta's skin glowed with soft, creamy olive tones and was much lighter than Isabel's. She slumped while Isabel sat up straight, ready for battle.

Isabel broke the silence: "Mija, they gave you all kinds of shit that messed up your body just to do that FBI shit on that woman so she could have *your* babies!"

"IVF not FBI," said Marta calmly. Normally she laughed at Isabel's malapropisms.

"Whatever," said Isabel undeterred. "FBI or IVF, the fuckin' result's the same. You is fucked up, mija, and you gotta do something about it! Hire a lawyer or something!" Isabel thought for a moment. "Or maybe," she suddenly offered, "maybe you can get on that show with what's his face . . . You know, that Jerry Springer guy. That'll embarrass the hospital and they'll throw money at you!"

Marta didn't want to hear any of this. *Next, on Jerry Springer: Stupid and gullible Chicana screws up her body because an ad made her cry! And who do we have waiting in the green room to meet her? The woman she helped, Patricia Novas-Hall, her beautiful twin girls, and her gabacho husband!* Marta need-ed comfort right then and not the type of advice being dispensed by her friend. She felt as though she had found out that she had six months to live. It wasn't that Marta knew that she wanted to be a mother, but she wanted to make the choice as any other woman would. Now a whole part of her life was ending—cut out like a tumor—and Isabel's comments weren't helping. But Marta knew that Isabel loved her and wanted to help.

"Can you have babies if you try right now?"

"My doctor said that the odds were extremely low and that it might be dangerous," said Marta almost in a monotone.

"You know that I've been in a lot of pain. My system's all messed up." She stood up. "Isabel, can I come over tonight and talk some more? I have to get to school right now. I have to meet Jaime for coffee. I need to tell him."

"Shit!" Isabel sputtered. "Mija, you haven't told Jaime yet? He's going to be so pissed! He's always talkin' about getting married to you and having tons of babies! *Shit!"*

Marta felt spent and empty. She put some money on the table. "Can I come by about nine tonight?"

Isabel stood up and hugged Marta. It created an odd tableau because Isabel towered over her friend and she had to hunch over to embrace Marta.

"I'm so sorry, mija," said Isabel. "I'm so sorry. Come by whenever you want. I love you."

Marta offered a wan smile. She turned and headed to the back door of the deli to get to the parking lot. Isabel stood with her hands on her hips and watched her friend walk away. Marta passed a table where Laura, the young mother, sat hugging her baby. Laura rested her lips on the baby's forehead while keeping an eye on her son, who was attempting to pour catsup on his plate. Marta's nostrils widened as she imagined smelling the baby's talcum and milky breath. She continued and pushed the glass door to get out of the deli. The door felt heavier than before and it let out a mournful creak. The sun shone hot and bright. As she walked to her car, Marta wrapped her arms around herself. Maybe, if she squeezed tightly enough, she could stop her body from changing. She knew she could stop it, somehow. She would not become an old woman. Not before her time. Not yet.

German Music

agoberto lets his metal cane slide from his short brown fingers and nestle with a sharp *clink* at the side of the LifeCycle recumbent bike. He lets out a sigh and a barely audible *¡Chingao!* through his perfectly aligned glistening white dentures as he lifts his weak leg over the spine of the LifeCycle. He slowly settles his round rump into the cushioned seat. With another sigh, Dagoberto straps his feet onto the pedals and starts his thrice-weekly workout ordered by Dr. Hager after the stroke. He snaps miniature headphones onto his ears, pushes a button on the CD player that hangs from his waistband, and closes his heavy-lidded eyes. Dagoberto's head starts to bob up and down to his secret beat. The room hums with the chatter and grunting of the usual Saturday morning gym rats.

"Whatcha listenin' to, Bert?"

Dagoberto almost jumps out of his seat with an *¡Híjole!* His eyes pop open and rest upon the visage of friend and fellow stroke victim Brian Reid.

"Didn't mean to scare you, Bert."

Dagoberto turns off the CD and brings the headphones down to his already sweaty, brawny neck.

"It's okay, Brian."

"So?"

"So what?"

"Whatcha listenin' to?"

"Oh." Dagoberto wipes his forehead with a small white towel. "German music."

"German music?" Brian tries to smile but his face droops so badly on the left side, it looks like he's about to cry.

"Yeah. Me prende."

"What?"

"I like it."

"Why?"

Dagoberto coughs. "It's all mi esposa listens to. She speaks German to me as much as she can."

"You understand German?"

"Some. From the war. From mi esposa."

Brian laughs. "She don't wanna learn Spanish?"

"What do you care? You don't speak it. Anyway, you know goddamn Germans. Stubborn gente."

"Why do you prefer German music?"

"I never said I preferred it. It's a change of pace from the usual shit."

Brian leans in, his breath heavy with morning coffee, his white face almost glowing. "Me, I like the classics. You know, Sinatra, Crosby, and a little bit of Sammy."

"Sammy?"

"Davis."

"Oh. That negrito sure could put on a pinche good show. Me and Christine saw him in Vegas in '65. Goddamn best show we ever saw. Shame he's dead."

"Yeah. Liked him on the Bob Hope specials."

Dagoberto shook his head. "Sammy never was on no pinche Hope special."

"Sure as shit he was. He even did that USO stuff."

"No!"

"That stroke screwed up your memory, Bert. Even got you listenin' to that damn German music!"

"I like to mix it up. Right now it's my thing. Reminds me of Mexican music. All that accordion. Best goddamn instrument. Muy suavecito."

"Then listen to Mexican music!"

Dagoberto grabs his headphones, plops them over his ears, and pushes the ON button. "Adiós, Brian."

"Good-bye, you jackass," whispers Brian with a crooked smile, knowing that Dagoberto can't hear him.

Dagoberto smiles back. "Adiós," he mouths through a smile. He closes his eyes. "Adiós, pinche pendejo."

THERE'S BEEN A SHOOTING

Your day is chugging along pretty well. You got your nine-year-old son to camp on time and now you click away on your computer drafting an opposition to a motion for a new trial in a nasty case you've just won. Most of your coworkers sit in the Ronald Reagan State Building's cafeteria eating lunch and tossing loving barbs at each other in the way only litigators can appreciate. You didn't join them because you had lunch plans at 1:00 with a former law clerk who was now a young attorney in a boutique Beverly Hills firm.

As you type, you decide that you could use a little jazz so you turn on your RCA clock radio. After a few moments of music, the disc jockey breaks in and says words that don't quite register: "shootings" and "North Valley Jewish Community Center" and "at least three children wounded" and "there may be more than one shooter." These words finally seep into your consciousness and you yell, "Oh my God!" and start to call your wife at work. No answer. Just voice mail. You leave a frantic message telling her what you've heard. You try her parents' house because they live near the Center. Your parents live too far. You reach your mother-in-law and tell her to get to the camp to find your son. You run out the door and head to the parking garage. You arrive at the car and your legs start to buckle so you lean onto the cool metal of your Honda Accord. You realize that you have not taken a breath since you left the building so you concentrate on breathing deeply while repeating to yourself, "I have to get to him." You feel in control again and get into the car to start your drive from downtown L.A. to Granada Hills not knowing.

As you break the speed limit and listen to the news, you remember when you studied for your conversion to Judaism. One day your rabbi asked you, "Why do you want to take on the mantle of a people who have been hated and slaughtered throughout history?" It was a good question but you offered a snappy answer: *I am Chicano. I know prejudice.* You acknowledge that you could think of little in history to compare to the horror of the Holocaust, but you could, at the very least, empathize with the Jewish people because of your own people's history. But now you wonder how you would answer the rabbi's question. Your mind is bouncing to unspeakable thoughts, images, sounds. *Is he dead?* You shake your head to clear your mind and you think of a song your son learned at camp last month, sung to the tune of "Louie, Louie" by the Kingsmen:

Pharaoh, Pharaoh.
Whoa baby, let my people go!
Yeah, yeah, yeah!

You try to conjure up the smell of your son's hair as you wonder if you and your wife have been made childless this hot August day.

SOURCE ACKNOWLEDGMENTS

The following stories appeared previously, sometimes in slightly different form, and are reprinted by permission of the author: "The Fox" in *Octavo* (fall 1999); "The Plumed Serpent of Los Angeles" in *Southern Cross Review* (November/December 1999), reprinted in *Fantasmas: Supernatural Stories by Mexican American Writers* (Bilingual Press, 2001); "The Horned Toad" in *Fables* (December 1999); "Señor Sánchez" in *Nemeton: A Fables Anthology* (Silver Lake Publishing, 2000); "Don de la Cruz and the Devil of Malibu" in *Exquisite Corpse* (February/March 2000); "Bender" in *The Pacific Review* (spring 2000); "Sight" in *MindKites* (spring 2000); "Buridan's Ass" in *The Vestal Review* (July 2000); "Black Box" in *Raven Electrick* (September 2000); "Eurt" in *The Paumanok Review* (winter 2000); "Muy Loca Girl" in *Southern Cross Review* (March/April 2001); "Devil Talk" in *Facets Magazine* (April 2001); "You're the Only One Here" in *The New Journal* (July 2001); "A Melancholy Chime" in *12gauge.com* (September 2001); "Ramona" in *Octavo* (March 2002); "Willie" in *In Posse Review* (July 2002); "On the Hill" in *LatinoLA* (August 2002); "La Guaca" in *The Vestal Review* (January 2003); "German Music" in *The Sidewalk's End* (September 2003); "Monk" in *In Posse Review* (September 2003); "Four Seasons" in *Tattoo Highway* (January 2004); and "Real Time" in *Homestead Review* (2004).